# The Allotments

*Jean Illingworth*

Clink
Street

*Published by Clink Street Publishing 2021*

*Copyright © 2021*

*First edition.*

*ISBN:*
*978-1-914498-15-2 - paperback*
*978-1-914498-16-9 - ebook*

*This book is dedicated to my late father, Leonard, and father-in-law, Jack, who both loved to garden.*

*Also dedicated to my dear husband, DJ, and to gardeners and allotment holders everywhere.*

# WINTER

# CHAPTER ONE

Josie ran her hand through her hair and gazed out across the allotments, each little plot subtly different from each other, like squares of a handmade quilt where each individual piece of fabric preserved the memory of the person who had once worn it.

At this time of year there wasn't much to see; bare soil white-crisped with frost, shapeless lumps of dormant vegetation, naked black branches scratching heavy white sky. But if you looked closer there was life there; tiny green shoots poking bravely through the frozen ground, tightly closed buds waiting on the branches, birds busy on the many birdfeeders hung in the trees. Her gentle movements around her little patch of land didn't startle the birds as they flew back and forth over her head, welcome colour and life in this monotone winter landscape.

Josie rubbed her cold hands together and grimaced, partly at the pain of arthritis in her fingers, always worse when cold, and partly at the crusting of mud that showered off them. She realised her short white hair would not only be standing on end but also streaked with mud, but shrugged, unconcerned: who was there to see her? Today, in that dead time between Christmas and New Year, she was alone, her fellow allotment holders wrapped warmly in the bosom of their families.

Josie picked up the bag of frost-sweetened parsnips that she had just dug up and walked home down the hill as the grey of the afternoon darkened. She was soon embraced by warm stone walls, the jumble of houses snaking up the hill from the square at the heart of the small moor-side town of Kirkby where she had lived all her life. Most houses had small Christmas trees displayed in brackets high above their doors, and the necklace of coloured lights sparkled and danced and made her smile.

She caught glimpses of happy families through windows as she passed, golden light spilling across the pavement and snatches of laugher or music jumbling together as she passed.

Her own home was dark and cold when she entered, but she soon had a fire roaring cheerfully and her parsnips roasting in the oven alongside the joint she had put in earlier. Pouring a large glass of red wine, she watched the firelight glow through it, its ruby glow rivalling the baubles on her small tree.

As she silently said goodbye to the old year and toasted the new one, Josie hoped she was ready for whatever it would bring.

# CHAPTER TWO

Josie sat in the doorway of her shed, a well-thumbed seed catalogue on her knee and a steaming mug of tea on an upturned plant pot next to her. It was very cold still, but a multi-coloured bobble hat her granddaughter had given her for Christmas and her late husband's plaid wool scarf were keeping her warm. She wasn't sure they went very well together, but she wore the scarf on all but the hottest of days, its hug like his arms around her still.

Josie sighed, thinking about Keith. The allotment had been their shared passion, and she still expected to look up from planting and see him tying up runner beans or holding up a fistful of bright carrots for her to admire. She always felt closest to him there, using the trowel his hands had held or deadheading the roses he had planted for her.

He had always liked this stage of the gardening year, planning what they would try new this year, the anticipation before the hard work of digging and planting. Josie still enjoyed the planning, but her favourite time of year was spring when the days were milder and the multi-coloured tulips danced below soft clouds of apple blossom.

"Fancy a piece of cake with that, Josie?" asked her allotment neighbour, Kara, proffering a tin over the hedge towards her.

"Only if you'll join me in a cup of tea to go with it," replied Josie with a smile.

"On my way," said Kara.

Josie clicked the kettle back on to boil and unfolded another rickety garden chair.

"I was baking for the school and thought I'd do a few extra," said Kara as Josie admired the delicate fairy cakes that tasted as good as they looked.

"Still fundraising, are they?" asked Josie with a grin. "Some things never change!"

Josie had been the Headmistress at the local primary school until her retirement five years previously and she still took a keen interest in the school. Sadly, Keith had passed away two years after her retirement, and they never had the chance to fulfil all the plans that they had made for after she left the demands of her job behind. She sometimes wished she was still working but had no idea how she had ever found time for it as she didn't seem to have a spare moment in her days.

"We are saving up for trip to Disneyland Paris in the summer," replied Kara. "We want to subsidise places for children whose parents can't afford it, so that everyone gets to go."

"What a great idea," said Josie, warmly. "Flamingo Land was the limit in my day, and the local print company paid for the coach, so it was very affordable for everyone, but Disneyland Paris sounds wonderful. I bet the children are excited!"

"Well, my two are," replied Kara. "Ronan is even eating all his vegetables in the hope he will grow tall enough before the summer to go on all the rides!"

The two friends laughed, Josie thinking of all the ploys she'd used with her own daughter to get her to eat healthily.

Whilst they chatted, Kara studied her friend surreptitiously, not having seen her since before Christmas. Apart from a ridiculous hat and the ever-present scarf, Josie was, as always, neatly turned out (her gardening clothes better that Kara's work clothes) but when you looked past that, Kara thought she looked a bit pale and a little thinner than when she had last seen her.

Kara had known Josie most of her life: she'd been her class teacher at the local school, and then Headmistress there when her own children went to the same school. As a small child, Kara had thought her teacher beautiful, and even now she was in her late sixties, Josie's face was still almost unlined, and her eyes a rich conker brown behind her glasses.

"Philip's given up his allotment," said Josie, nodding towards the allotment on the other side of Kara's.

"Ah, I thought it was getting a bit much for him," replied Kara. "Whoever gets it is very lucky; been a lot of manure dug into that soil over the years!"

"Don't I know it" replied Josie, thinking of how the smell had hung like a malevolent presence over the allotments for weeks ever year.

"I wonder who will get it?" mused Kara.

"Ah, well, I can tell you that," said Josie, who was the Chair of the Allotment Association.

"Thought so," said Kara with a grin. "I'm hoping it's an attractive single man…"

"Well, I don't know about that, but it is a man. Hugo Haywood-Smith his name is, but I know nothing else about him, apart from he'd been on the waiting list for quite some time."

"Sound posh," said Kara pulling a face. "I need someone who won't mind getting their hands dirty."

"He'll certainly have to do that, or there is no point him getting an allotment," replied Josie with a laugh. "Besides, you've always just got on and done what ever needed doing without any help!"

"Yes, but it would be nice not to always have to do so," said Kara glumly.

Josie squeezed Kara's hand, knowing how difficult it was for Kara bringing up two children alone since her divorce.

"When would you have time for a relationship anyway?" asked Josie with a laugh.

"I wasn't thinking about a relationship, just some hot sex between my stints at the food bank and work at the RSPCA."

"You still wouldn't have time," said Josie, trying not to blush at Kara's frankness. "Don't forget you run the Friends of the School as well as chauffeuring the children to their many afterschool clubs. Oh, and then there's the allotment," she added.

"Hmm, I suppose you're right, I don't have time even for a quickie! But you might. Hugo sounds like more your generation…," said Kara.

Josie spluttered on her last mouthful of tea, liquid and cake crumbs going everywhere.

"Me!" she gasped, hoping Kara would think her red face was from nearly choking and not from embarrassment. "Oh no, I'm past all that. After forty years of marriage, it's nice to have a bit of time for myself."

"Never say never, Josie," said Kara with a wicked grin, as she picked up the cake tin and headed back to her own side of the hedge.

Shaking her head to get rid of the unwanted images Kara had put in there, Josie watched her go, and thought how pretty she looked with her curvy figure and waves of long, auburn hair tumbling out from under a bobble hat that was even more colourful that her own.

# CHAPTER THREE

A heavy fall of snow kept Josie away from her allotment for a few days. She felt uncharacteristically on edge, unable to settle to any task, but a Skype call to her daughter Amy in Australia cheered her up. Amy took her phone outside so that Josie could see her beautiful granddaughter, Mollie, running round their large garden in the sunshine with her new puppy. Mollie was having far too much fun to stop and talk to her, just shouted, "Hi Grandma," and waved each time she dashed past the phone.

Once the call finished, the house felt too quiet, so Josie decided she would walk up to the allotments and check everything was okay. As she stepped outside the cold air took her breath away, but she carried on, sticking to the main road that had been gritted and avoiding the treacherous churned-up snow on the pavement.

The undisturbed snow blanketing the allotments gave it a magical feel, the scruffy huts, tatty water buts and rusty wheelbarrows all a uniform white. A lone sunflower stalk, left to feed the birds, stood sentinel at the entrance, its dried seed head stark black against the whiteness. Here and there a row of overwintering red cabbages or stalks of still green Brussel sprouts poked through the snow giving a welcome splash of colour.

Josie's stout boots crunched through the crisp snow as she made her way to her hut, intent on filling up her birdfeeders. She was surprised to see a few other tracks in the snow, not just birds and possibly a fox, but a man's footprints back and forth along some of the paths. No one was in sight, so after calling out "Hello" and getting no answer, Josie completed her task and then headed home, eager for a hot cup of soup to warm her up.

A week later, every trace of the snow was gone, replaced by almost warm sunshine and blue skies. Josie was at her allotment early and had been giving everything a good tidy up, cleaning out the shed and greenhouse, and rubbing linseed oil into the wooden handles of her gardening tools. She was just cleaning the windows of her greenhouse with diluted vinegar when she noticed a man working at the next but one allotment.

"I'll go and say 'Hello' once I've finished this," she thought, but by the time she'd rinsed everything down he was gone.

"Knock, knock," said a male voice a few minutes later. Josie turned with a smile of welcome and recognised her old friend, and the Society's Treasurer, John.

"Hello John, I thought you might have been Hugo, our mysterious new allotment holder. Have you met him yet?" she said.

"No, not yet, but I see he's made a good start already," said John.

"Oh good. And how are you John: enjoying this better weather?" asked Josie.

"Well, I'm not sure. Either I'm imagining things, or some of my winter vegetables are disappearing!" he replied.

"Oh, I hope we haven't got a problem with rats again," said Josie with a frown.

"Rats of the two-legged variety, Josie, I'm starting to think," said John. "Several of the vegetable I'd left in to overwinter have vanished over the last week or so, and some of the other allotment holders are reporting the same."

"Oh no," said Josie. "We've never had that before. As you know, we had a problem with shed break-in's a few years ago, with easy to sell items going, but no one's ever stolen produce. Lovely as your veg is, John, I can't see it being traded on the black market!"

"No," replied John with a wry smile. "We need to get to the bottom of it now, before everyone is busy planting their summer and autumn crops; that's a lot of work to then not have a full harvest at the end."

"Yes indeed," said Josie with a frown. "I'll email everyone to tell them to be vigilant and see if anyone can throw some light on what's going on."

After John had gone, Josie sat for a while in her shed, perturbed at what John had told her. Crime in the area was very low, and the allotment holders a close community, all of whom she knew and trusted. She hoped John had been mistaken but knew that was unlikely as John was very meticulous, and probably kept a spreadsheet detailing the exact number of each parsnip or leek he had planted!

Dispirited, Josie decided to finish up for the day, for once locking her shed, but stopping short of counting her vegetables. As she walked down the hill, she noticed a handwritten poster fastened to a lamp post and stopped to read it.

"Missing golden-brown cat with distinctive black markings. Please check your sheds," it read followed by a phone number.

"That's the third missing cat poster I've seen in the last few weeks," thought Josie, shaking her head and deciding she would add the plea to check sheds to her email to all allotment holders.

# CHAPTER FOUR

John stood for a while and surveyed his plot. Whoever had been stealing his veg didn't like Brussel sprouts as they were untouched, but some leeks, kale, cabbage, parsnips and broad beans had definitely gone. The thief had been careful not to pull up plants next to each other, so that to a less observant man than him, the theft might have gone unnoticed. In fact, his neighbouring allotment holders hadn't noticed similar thefts until he'd asked them to check.

It wasn't the value of the produce that bothered him – at most they were worth a few pounds – but the fact that someone had been there. It felt like sacrilege, a violation of a sacred space. Since Mary had become ill, the allotment had become his sanctuary, somewhere he could come for a precious couple of hours whilst the carer was with her, somewhere he felt in control.

In the early days of Mary's illness, before she became wheelchair bound, she would sit on the bench in the lea of the shed where it was warmed by the sun but out of the wind, and read whilst he pottered about the allotment. He would look up from digging and see her watching him, her hair a sunlight halo and her smile even warmer than the sun. She would blow him a kiss and then go back to her book, and when he stopped for a mug of tea with her, she would tell him about the characters in the story and he would tell her about the plants he had put in.

She would tease him about his straight rows and joke that his vegetables would not dare to be anything less than perfect and he would laugh with her, admitting he was a bit of a control freak. But now, the one thing he couldn't control was the only thing that really mattered, and every day he lost a little more of the only women he had ever loved. The bench was still there, but John never sat there, never stopped for tea, just worked hard for a couple of hours until he was calm, taking his frustration at Mary's illness out on the soil.

Glancing at his watch he realised he had stayed too long and must hurry home, but just then a ray of sunlight spotlighted the bench and he stopped and stared into it, fancying he could see Mary sitting there, could see her sweet smile and hear her laughter. He shook his head to clear it, cross with himself for being so fanciful. He surreptitiously wiped a tear from his eye, blew his nose loudly and then double-checked the locks on his shed.

As he left the allotments, he closed the padlock on the gate and shook the chain to ensure it was tight. All the allotment holders knew the combination for the padlock, so whoever was getting in must be climbing over the gate. As he walked home with a heavy heart, John made a mental note to add the possibility of CCTV to the agenda for the next AGM.

# CHAPTER FIVE

Kara read Josie's email to all allotment holders and laughed. Only John would have noticed a few vegetables were missing! Still, it wasn't nice to think that someone was stealing the fruits of their hard labour.

Kara knew her allotment wasn't the tidiest or the most productive, but it was important to her. She had 'inherited' it from her dad, and he still popped round regularly to give her advice, or just chat with her and his old friends the other allotment holders.

On the weekends when she had the children, if the weather was dry, she's taken them to the allotment where each of them had their own mini plots, just like she and her sisters had when they were small. Ronan's was mainly dedicated to creating habitats for insects, and Lily only wanted to plant 'pretty flowers', but it was a great excuse to get them outside and involved in nature. They would also eat vegetables if they came from the allotment, even though they wouldn't touch them in their school dinners.

During the week Kara could rarely get there, but on the weekends that her ex-husband, Andy, had the children, she could spend all day at the allotment. With one thing and another it had been over two weeks since she'd been there, and worried, not about missing cabbages but about locked-in cats, Kara decided to pop in quickly before she picked the kids up from school.

Arriving at her allotment, she could see how much everything, especially the weeds, had come on with the slightly warmer weather of the last few days. Kara resolved to make time for the allotment this weekend before everything got too out of hand.

The shed door was unlocked, but that didn't surprise her as she often forgot to lock it, but the sleeping bag and camping stove inside were a bit of a shock. Kara stepped back and looked around her, but there was no one lurking about. The padlock was on the shelf, and she picked it up, but before she clipped it onto the hasp, she hesitated: what if the person had nowhere else to sleep?

Volunteering at the food bank as she did, she knew how tough things were currently for a lot of people, and despite today's sunshine, it was still very cold especially at night if you were a rough sleeper. She knew her dad wouldn't approve, but she put the padlock back on the shelf, adding to it the KitKat she had in her pocket, and just pulled the door to.

The weekend came, and with the kids at their dads, Kara had all day free to clear the weeds and get the soil dug over ready for planting or she'd have no vegetables this year. She didn't have a greenhouse, so as soon as the soil had warmed up a little, she'd be planting her early crops direct into the soil, so it would be good to get it ready.

Hoping to see Josie and see if anyone had found the missing cat, she'd brought a tin of homemade brownies to share, her 'signature' bake and Josie's favourite. Josie wasn't around so Kara went straight to her plot, and with some trepidation opened the door to the shed. No one was in inside, and Kara let out the breath she didn't realise she was holding, but then realised that the sleeping bag and camping stove were still there.

She whirled around to check that no one had come in behind her and saw instead a jam jar full of snowdrops on the shelf where she'd left the KitKat earlier in the week. An old seed packet was leaned against it with the words 'thank you' written across it. Kara picked the jar up and sniffed the flowers, inhaling the faint fresh green smell: the word 'hope' popped into her head, and she remembered that was what snowdrops symbolised.

As Kara got on with the hard work of digging over the soil, she kept looking around for her mystery 'guest' but saw no one she didn't already know apart from Hugo, the new allotment holder. She gave him a wave and then grinned when he waved back, remembering the conversation she'd had with Josie; he was old enough to be her father. He did, however, look really nice, with a kind 'lived-in' face and thick, wavey grey hair. He was wearing red corduroy trousers tucked into his wellies and a neatly pressed checked shirt under a green body warmer and looked remarkably clean for someone busy digging muck.

Kara glanced down at her old jeans and baggy jumper and thought she'd wait till she was a bit more presentable before introducing herself. She knew her hair needed a wash and was just scrapped back in a ponytail out of the way, but knowing she was on her own all weekend, there hadn't been any point making an effort.

Kara had noticed earlier some bags of horse manure left by the local stables under the 'Swaps' bench and went to fetch some to improve her soil. She was lucky that the plot she had inherited was towards the bottom of the allotments and the soil was reasonably good. Towards the top end the soil was heavy, full of clay, which got waterlogged when it rained and cracked and dry when it was sunny. New allotment holders allocated those plots usually swapped for the better plots lower down as soon as any became available.

It was a struggle to lift the heavy, slippery bag of manure so she had to hug it to her chest, the pungent odour right under her nose making her feel sick. She knew it was sexist, but at times like this she missed her ex-husband who had always been good at the macho things, even if he hadn't been very good at being faithful. Having struggled with one bag, Kara decided to wait until she could borrow a wheelbarrow to fetch more. Her own wheelbarrow had dropped to bits last summer, and money being tight, she'd not got around to buying another one yet.

Stopping to stretch her back and survey her handiwork, Kara thought glumly it didn't look much better, and she certainly looked worse, her jumper covered in manure and curls of hair that had escaped the ponytail hanging around her sweaty face. Having wiped the worst of the mud off her hands onto her jeans, Kara rewarded herself with a brownie, sighing with satisfaction as the rich chocolate melted on her tongue.

"Who needs sex when you have chocolate?" she murmured to herself.

She hadn't meant to speak out loud, and looked around quickly, embarrassed, having a distinct feeling she was being watched. However, as the days were short still and the afternoon already growing cold, the allotments were deserted. She helped herself to another brownie and then put the lid firmly back on the tin, knowing that comfort eating was not going to help her slim down in order to, perhaps, attract a new man.

Kara placed the tin on the self in the shed and picked up her jam jar of snowdrops before going home, once again leaving the shed unlocked.

# CHAPTER SIX

From his hiding place amongst the trees bordering the allotments, Jack watched Kara. When she'd come to the shed a few days ago, he expected to return once she had gone and find his sleeping bag thrown out and the shed locked. Finding it still unlocked, and a chocolate bar left for him had brought tears to his eyes - it was the first bit of kindness he had experienced in a long time.

Seeing her arch her back, her hair in glorious disarray and her face and clothing streaked with mud, he thought she was very beautiful. Watching her eat the cake with a look of unrestrained pleasure on her face made him realise that he hadn't felt joy for a very long time. The only thing he had felt was numb, deliberately not letting himself think or feel anything, just concentrating on getting through the day with as little contact with other people as he could manage.

At the beginning of the winter he had slept in a hostel, but before long the press of people around him and the weight of all their problems began to suffocate him and he had to get away and be on his own again. He had felt the need to get out of the city too, so day by day he walked north, heading towards the moors and the big skies.

He hadn't bargained on the unavailability of places to sleep and the difficulty in finding food: in the city there were always doorways sheltered from the wind and bins overflowing with discarded takeaways. Snow and hunger drove him to shelter in the allotments, and although he didn't like to steal, he didn't think anyone would miss a few vegetables when there were so many just left there in the ground to rot.

Returning to the shed again once the lady had left, he couldn't believe his luck when he looked in the tin and saw the delicious looking brownies. This second act of kindness somehow unlocked a door in his mind he had not opened in a long time, and, pulling his sleeping bag around him in the dark, he allowed his mind to wander back to a time before everything changed.

He and Julie had married young, childhood sweethearts who had never been out with anyone else. They hadn't much money, but that didn't matter, they were happy in their little rented flat, saving hard for a house of their own. Julie was training to be a nurse, studying between shifts, and he worked two jobs, so they didn't have a lot of time together, and rarely went out. Jack knew it wasn't much fun, but he was focused on the goal of getting their own house, and thought Julie was too.

But that future changed the day he came home from work early, his hands full of bags of ingredients for a special meal he planned to cook to celebrate a promotion he'd been given at work. Dumping the bags in the hall, he pulled a bottle of prosecco from them and dashed upstairs to find her. He could hear movement in their bedroom, and headed there, opening the door quietly in order to surprise her.

Julie didn't see him, her eyes closed in ecstasy, and her lover didn't see him either, his back to the door as his naked body pumped rhythmically into hers.

Jack turned and ran down the stairs, out the front door and just kept running till he couldn't run any more, trying to get away from the image seared onto his eyeballs. Something in him shattered, shut down to shut it out, and when he woke the next morning, huddled in a doorway, his mind was blank. With no life of his own now, he fell into the cracks between other people's lives, unseen and unseeing. A homeless man soon becomes invisible, people passing by pretending they didn't see him. If anyone was looking for him, they never found him, and he drifted in time and place, learning the skills of survival whilst forgetting everything else.

Jack hadn't realised he was crying, until the tears splashed onto his hands, leaving a track through the grime. He felt something shift inside him and knew he was ready to let go of the pain, to mourn the life with Julie he had lost. Eventually his sobs ceased, and with a new clarity he could see that she hadn't been happy, and neither had he really. They were just a habit, a life they had fallen into not realising they had fallen out of love. That understanding freed him, and he realised he was ready to live again, move out of this self-imposed half-life and into the sun again.

Exhausted but calm, he ate three brownies in a row, the sugar hit being what he needed just then. He thought they were the best thing he had ever tasted and he silently thanked the kind lady who had baked them. For the first time in a very long time, he fell straight asleep, and despite the cold, slept solidly until the sunrise woke him.

Jack watched out of the hut window at a new day dawning and felt like his new life was just beginning.

# CHAPTER SEVEN

Josie picked up her fork and began to dig over her vegetable beds, digging in plenty of compost from her own compost heap. She wasn't a vain person, but she was very proud of her compost. After many years of disastrous attempts at compost making that ended up either slimy or terribly smelly, she had somehow got it right. It was such a small thing to give her joy, but it did, each spade full of rich, brown crumbly soil with its earthy smell that brought back memories of woodland walks and made her happy.

Josie wasn't very good at baking cakes, but she always thought compost making was like following a cake recipe, getting the right mix of ingredients (plenty of dry brown materiel mixed in with the fresh green), chopping it up small (no large branches), not letting it get too dry, and mixing it well. She had discovered that lifting and turning the material regularly to bring in more oxygen was important, otherwise it went cold and stopped rotting. She always added a large dollop of already made compost to a new heap as it was full of micro-organisms that she fancied would start the composting process quickly – a little like sourdough starter when bread making.

The final important step was to keep the heap covered to keep in the warmth. Josie used a piece of the old carpet that had been in her house when she and Keith had bought it. It was garish, with swirls of orange and brown and they had replaced it as soon as they could afford to, but it made her smile, reminding her of the happy times they had spent making the house their own.

As she dug, Josie let her mind wander everywhere and nowhere. Gardening was like that; meditative. Gardeners had been practising 'mindfulness' for a very long time before it became trendy. Somehow, however, her mind returned to Kara's silly comments a few weeks ago. She was pretty sure she didn't miss sex, but maybe, just maybe, she did miss companionship.

Not the day-to-day interactions that she had plenty of at the allotments and local shops, but someone to share the ups and downs of each day with, who wouldn't judge her if she had a moan about someone who had annoyed her, who would rub her back when it ached or just make her a cup of tea when she needed one without being asked.

Tired with digging, Josie made a cup of tea for herself and sat alone just inside the entrance to her shed to drink it. She could see someone digging over Kara's plot and was envious of his energy and enthusiasm. She was pleased Kara was getting some help as she was always going out of her way to help others, but with her back aching and her hands sore, today she wished she had someone to help her too.

Too tired to do anything more energetic, Josie retired to her potting shed for the easier task of planting seeds of early peas, broad beans, cabbage and lettuce, ready to plant out once the soil was warmer.

As the evening started to close in and she made her way slowly back down the hill to home, Josie noticed another poster for a missing cat. After her email a few weeks ago, most of the allotment holders had replied to say they had checked their sheds and had not found any cats. Although she had done her bit, Josie still couldn't help worrying about it.

When her daughter had been small, they had had a lovely cat, a common-or-garden moggy, but with silky-soft fur and a big personality. She was long gone, and Josie hadn't thought about her for a while, but maybe she ought to get herself a cat again, some company and someone who needed her. She laughed at the thought of a cat needing her, knowing cats didn't need humans, they just used them and would happily move onto someone else if they offered them a cushier life. Maybe that was what the local cats had done – just moved to a new house with no thought for their poor owners worrying about them.

Overnight there was a return to sub-zero temperatures and the next morning the allotments were white with frost, each leaf and blade of grass edged with crystals that shimmered in the weak sunlight. The ground was too hard to plant, so, having checked the few outside plants were well covered in fleece to protect them, there was nothing else she could do. Josie decided to check the pipes in the allotment's communal toilet were well wrapped up too and then go home again, reckoning that walking up the hill and back counted as her daily exercise anyway.

She was surprised to see Kara standing rock still in her allotment staring at the earth, her hands on her hips and her breath a white plume hanging in the frosty air. She was wearing a bright pink bobble hat from which her lovely auburn curls had escaped and her cheeks were flushed with the cold. She brought welcome colour to the muted landscape and although she had a perplexed look on her face, Josie though she looked very pretty.

"Everything alright, Kara?" asked Josie, and Kara jumped at the sound of her voice.

"More than alright, Josie," replied Kara, "just look at this!"

Josie looked at the earth that Kara was pointing to. It had been dug and dug again so that the soil was loose and free of any large lumps. Although covered in a crisp layer of frost, Josie could see a lot of darker manure evenly spread throughout the soil and wished her own plot was as well prepared.

"Wow Kara, that looks wonderful. Your gardener has done a brilliant job. Was he expensive, because if not, I think I could do with some help too?"

"It didn't cost me anything Josie," replied Kara. "I haven't been up for a week and somehow this has just happened! Gardening fairies perhaps?"

"Not fairies," laughed Josie, "but there was a man working diligently here yesterday."

Kara started at her with wide eyes.

"What did he look like?" she asked.

"Well, I was a way off, and it was difficult to tell due to his beard, but he looked to be young – probably around your age Kara," replied Josie.

"He was very thin, with longish hair tied back in a ponytail and, well, scruffy," she continued, ignoring Kara's snort of amusement at being called young.

"But then you wouldn't be smartly dressed if you planned to dig all day, would you?" added Josie, realising she had sounded snobby.

Kara looked at Josie with amusement. She had never seen Josie look anything other than clean and neat, no matter what mucky job she was tackling. Looking at her in the cold winter light, Kara realised that Josie was looking really tired and even thinner than when she'd seen her a few weeks ago. She hoped that Josie was looking after herself, as not only was she very fond of her, but they all relied on her to ensure that the allotments were well managed and the local council, who owned the land, where happy with everything.

"Do you know who it was, Kara?" asked Josie.

"No, it's not someone I know, but I think I have an idea who it *could* be," replied Kara, slowly.

"Well, if you find out, send him my way won't you," said Josie with a laugh, before waving goodbye and making her way home.

# CHAPTER EIGHT

Kara opened the door to the shed slowly and could see a huddled shape in the corner.

"Hi," she said softly, not wanting to startle him.

Jack leapt up, or at least tried to, but his aching back made fast movement difficult.

"I'm sorry," he said, "I know I shouldn't be here. I'll just gather up my stuff and I'll be out of here."

Kara looked at the ice on the inside of the window, at the man shuffling about in obvious pain and at his few sparse possessions.

"Well, you can't stay here," she said.

"No, I know that," he said, shoving his thin sleeping bag into an old rucksack as fast as he could. He looked round to see if he had missed anything, and seeing the cake tin, picked it up and held it to his chest for a moment before holding it out towards Kara.

"Thank you for the brownies," he said, looking directly at her. "They were delicious."

For the first time, Kara got the chance to have a good look at him. Josie had been right, he was about her age, and needed a good haircut and beard trim, but underneath all that hair was a face that would have been handsome if it hadn't been so thin. The man smiled at the memory of the sweet cakes, changing his face completely, and Kara got a glimpse of the man he had once been, or perhaps the man he was going to be. His eyes were a clear grey and held memories of pain, and Kara realised she was staring into them unmoving and was blocking his exit from the shed.

"I'll be on my way now," he said. "Sorry for sleeping here without asking."

"No, what I mean is you can't stay *here*," said Kara, indicating the frozen window and the frost covered allotments beyond. "It's going to be even colder tonight, and I don't want to come back tomorrow and find you've died of hypothermia overnight!" explained Kara. "Let me make a few calls and I'll find you some temporary accommodation," she continued.

"You'd do that for me?" he said in amazement.

"It's not much in return for all your hard work digging: it was you, wasn't it?"

"Well, yes, but that was just as a thank you," he replied, looking at his feet.

"Well, it's me that needs to thank you," replied Kara. "You've saved me a lot of work, and I'm really grateful, so the very least I can do is call in a few favours."

They introduced each other and then Kara handed Jack a flask of hot soup, and whilst he warmed his hands around a mug of it, she stepped outside to use her mobile. For some reason she couldn't explain, she instinctively trusted him and felt bad not just taking him back to her house, even if only for one night, but with children in the house it wasn't a risk she could take.

Through her work at the food bank, Kara had lots of useful contacts and it didn't take long to find him a room in a local bed and breakfast funded by the church outreach programme.

Whilst she drove him the short distance there, Kara mentioned that other allotment holders might be grateful for some help and would happily pay for it.

Kara left Jack at the B&B, clutching an old receipt with her phone number scrawled on it. He had a warm bed for the night, the possibility of paid work and, perhaps, just perhaps, a new friend.

His new life was beginning.

# CHAPTER NINE

Josie couldn't sleep. Something about the missing cats was worrying her. She didn't know why she couldn't let it go as it was nothing to do with her, but it just kept going round in her head.

Sighing, she got out and bed, wrapped a warm wool shawl around her shoulders before switching her PC on to boot up. It was ancient and needed a while to get going. 'A bit like me,' she thought, as she made herself a cup of hot chocolate.

As she sipped her drink, she opened the Kirkby Facebook page and skimmed through the entries for the last few months. She wasn't one for social media, and was astonished at the trivia people posted, but was also touched at the myriad of small acts of kindness in her local community. There were accounts of meals delivered to a sick neighbour, a dropped wallet returned, escaped dogs captured and held safe till their owners could be found, charity fundraising events, warnings to avoid an icy road… and people searching sheds and outbuildings for lost cats. Lots of missing cats, far more than the ones she had noticed recently.

Josie copied each cat's image and dropped them all onto a blank document side by side. "Well, well, well," she said to herself, looking at her handiwork. A pattern was emerging. At first glance, all the cats looked like ordinary tabby cats but with a slightly wilder appearance. But when you looked closer, all had distinctive dark markings, some almost leopard like, with smallish ears and black lines around their eyes as if they were wearing kohl.

Josie opened Google and, although they were not all the same colour, within minutes she was pretty certain they were all Bengal cats. She looked up breeders, and noted there was a local one, which might account for the amount of them owned locally. They were very beautiful, especially as kittens, and Josie briefly considered getting one for herself until she saw the price; £500 – £1200 per cat!

But surely, if they had been stolen, such valuable pets would be chipped, making it difficult to sell them on? Josie went back to the local breeder's website to get the phone number, having decided she would ring them in the morning to have a chat and see if they had any ideas. The name of the breeder, Sean Watson, was familiar to her, and after pondering a moment, she realised he was an allotment holder, but not one she knew well. Josie resolved to go and see him the next day, and, having at least moved a step nearer to solving the mystery, she went back to bed and slept well.

The next morning, whilst enjoying her second cup of tea, Josie opened up her allotment files and identified which plot was his. The plot was right at the top, bordering the woods. Which explained why she never saw much of him, as there was a short cut to that corner through the woods from a nearby road. According to the file, he'd had that plot a long time, which surprised her as it was not a good plot for growing vegetables, being overshadowed by large trees.

It was raining lightly but a little warmer as Josie walked up the hill, past her own plot and on towards Sean's. It was unlikely he'd be there, but worth a try to seek his advice as a fellow allotment holder rather than ring him up cold.

Josie had forgotten that there was a small barn-like building at the edge of Sean's plot, possibly an old stable or carriage house building from when the allotment land was the grounds of the Kirkby Manor. The manor house was still there but was now converted into flats with a view of the allotments rather than the previous landscaped gardens.

The barn was built of stone with solid wooden doors fitted with a stout padlock. Nothing appeared to have been planted in the allotment for a long time and the weeds had taken over and were spreading into the neighbouring plots. Actually, the neighbouring plot didn't look like it had been tended for a long time either; Josie tutted, knowing they had a waiting list for plots if someone wasn't bothering to use it.

Sean wasn't there, but Josie decided to check the barn for stray cats before going to her own plot where she'd make another cup of tea and then ring him from her mobile. She was surprised to find that the windows were boarded up on the inside, but between the boards tiny gleams of light shone out into the overcast day.

"He must have left the light on when he last locked up," she thought, but sensing movement inside, and having a sudden horror he'd somehow locked himself in, she knocked on the window. She heard a scrambling, and something being knocked over, and then, very clearly, miaowing. The poor cat must have been locked in, and Sean was perhaps away, or had missed her email and hadn't been up to check.

Josie leaned closer to the window and knocked again. The miaowing was louder and Josie realised that it was more than one cat as several different plaintive voices responded to her knock. Josie's blood ran cold as she realised this couldn't be an accidental locking in. Surely the cat breeder wasn't using his allotment for his business? His website showed a cosy kitchen with well looked after cats in a cute basket in front of a fire, not a cold and lonely shed in a forgotten corner of the allotments.

Josie tried the padlock on the door, but it was solidly locked. The miaowing grew louder as she rattled the door and Josie found herself getting upset at the thought of the cats stuck inside alone in the cold. She took out her phone to ring Sean and give him a piece of her mind, but then changed her mind and selected the number for Angie, the local community constable. Angie told her to go and wait at her own plot and said she'd be there as soon as she could, but it was likely to be later that afternoon.

Back in her shed and warming her hands around her mug of tea, Josie felt a bit calmer but decided she couldn't wait that long and rang Kara.

"Hi Josie," said Kara, on answering the phone. "Can't chat now, I'm at work, but there is something I want to speak to you about, so can I come and see you once my shift is finished?"

"Of course, but it's a work matter, I think, that I've rung you about," replied Josie.

Once Josie had explained the situation there was a moment's silence, and then Kara simply said, "I'm on my way," before hanging up.

Less than 30 minutes later, Kara's RSPCA van screeched to a halt and she jumped out, brandishing a large pair of bolt cutters. Barely greeting Josie, she marched up to Sean's plot, a murderous look on her face.

"Hang on Kara," said Josie, out of breath with trying to keep up. "Hadn't we better wait for Angie? Isn't it criminal damage if we cut the padlock off?"

"Probably," answered Josie to both questions but didn't pause for a moment in her mission.

Before Josie could stop her, the bolt cutters were around the padlock and Kara was closing them on it with all her strength. The broken padlock fell to the ground, and Kara opened the door a crack and peered inside, swearing loudly at what she could see. Josie couldn't see past her, but an awful smell reached her nostrils: Josie recognised it as the stench of a cat tray that needed changing, but this was a thousand times worse, mixed with the awful smell of decay.

Kara closed the door gently and turned to Josie, a stricken look on her face.

"Will you ring Angie and tell her I need her to send someone here, right now, to gather evidence for a potential animal cruelty prosecution," she said calmly, before ringing her colleagues at the local RSPCA and asking for assistance.

With the police on their way to witness and photograph what was inside the building, Kara reopened the door. Inside were eight or more once beautiful Bengal cats, each tethered to posts fixed into the floor at intervals. Around them were dozens of kittens, some alive and some dead. There was food, but it was rancid and covered in flies, and although each cat had a water bowl within reach, the water was soiled and, in one case, it had been knocked over leaving the cat without any.

"Josie, please will you fetch some water?" said Kara.

Josie was bit old for running, but she did, returning with a full watering can as fast as she could. Whilst Kara checked each cat in turn, Josie rinsed and filled the water bowls. One dehydrated cat looked at her listlessly but didn't move, and Josie dipped her finger into the bowl and dripped a little water onto the cat's mouth. The cat barely responded, but Josie kept trying, stroking the cat's head gently with one hand and talking to it softly whist continuing to drip water onto her mouth. Then the cat's pink tongue came out, and Josie dripped more onto that until the cat gave a little miaow of thanks before struggling up to lap up a little of the water herself.

"That's probably enough water for now, Josie," said Kara coming up behind her and squeezing her shoulder. "We'll put her on a drip as soon as we get her back."

Josie looked up, her eyes full of tears, and realised that the barn was filling up with police and Kara's RSPCA colleagues bringing cat carriers. She went outside to get out of their way and watched as they trudged back and forth carrying the cats to their vans. Soon all the living cats and kittens were on their way to the RSPCA 'hospital', Kara taking her own precious load after giving Josie a quick hug.

The police finished taking photographs and asked Josie to secure the shed, if she could, as they may need to come back later. They told her that an RSPCA Inspector would be in touch shortly to take a statement off her, and then they left her, alone with the dead kittens, the stench and despair in her heart.

# CHAPTER TEN

Kara had forgotten all about Jack in the trauma of the day and was just making the children's tea when her mobile rung.

"Sorry to trouble you Kara, but I just wanted to thank you for everything," said Jack.

"Don't be daft, I did very little," replied Kara, holding the phone between her ear and her shoulder whilst tipping oven chips onto a baking try. "How's your day been?"

"Good. Strange. Different, but good different," replied Jack uncertainly. "I'd forgotten how nice it was to sleep in a comfortable bed and wake up warm and safe. I wanted to stay in bed all day!"

"Why didn't you then?" asked Kara, knowing her fantasy was to do just that, if she didn't have children, work, responsibilities...

"Well, I'd arranged to meet with one of the outreach volunteers and he helped me fill in forms for benefits. He warned me that it could take some time, especially as I have no ID, so I've been out looking for work," replied Jack.

"Did you find any?" asked Kara, forgetting how difficult her day had been in the face of his problems.

"Not yet," he said. "You mentioned someone might need some help at the allotments?"

"Yes, I'm sorry, I meant to ask her, but, well, something came up," she said, not wanting to burden him with the horrors of her day.

"No problem," he said crestfallen.

"I'll ring her now and call you back. What's your number?" said Kara.

"I don't have one," replied Jack, "I'm just borrowing the landlady's phone, but it wouldn't be fair to trouble her again."

"Gosh, I can't imagine not having a phone. Look, if you don't mind sausage, chips and beans with the kids, why don't you come straight round here and I can ring Josie whilst it's cooking?"

"Really? Are you sure?" asked Jack.

Josie laughed and reassured him, then gave him directions from his nearby B&B. She quickly tipped some more chips onto the tray and popped a couple more sausages into the pan and whilst she stirred that one handed, she rang Josie.

Josie's first question was about the welfare of the cats and kittens, and Kara quickly reassured her that they were all doing well. With Jack due imminently, Kara cut the call short, promising Josie she'd come and see her tomorrow and talk it all thorough.

"Just one thing: can I bring someone with me? I found the person who'd dug my garden for me, and, well, he could do with a bit of help turning his life around and a little bit of paid work would be a good start," she told Josie.

"Any friend of yours is welcome, Kara, but if there is the added bonus of him digging my garden over for me, he is especially welcome!" replied Josie.

They said goodbye just as the doorbell rang, and Josie quickly turned off the sausages, which were a little burnt and went to answer the door. Jack had shaved off his beard, his hair was clean and neatly tied back and he was wearing a deep blue jumper that really suited him. Kara stared at him in surprise.

"Gosh, you look different" said Kara. "I barely recognised you!"

"It's amazing what a hot shower, a shave and a jumper liberated from the church's jumble pile can do," said Jack with a shy smile. "I certainly feel like I'm a new man."

Kara realised she was gazing at the nice face now revealed and turned away in confusion. The children came bounding down the stairs and the moment passed, and soon they were all tucking into their tea. Jack finished first, and Kara wondered if he'd had anything else to eat all day, so, much to the children's delight, declared there was pudding, and served up a lemon drizzle cake that she'd baked for the school fundraiser.

Jack happily accepted a second slice, and smiled his thanks, before concentrating on eating every last crumb. He seemed to be getting on really well with the kids, asking them about school, favourite books and TV programmes and Kara wondered if he'd had his own kids in a previous life.

The evening flew by, and it was only when Lily started to nod off that Kara realised the time and rushed them upstairs to bed. When she returned, Jack had washed up and was just putting on his torn, and to be honest, slightly smelly, old coat.

He was just thanking her for a wonderful meal when she had a thought.

"Hang on a moment, Jack," she said before dashing back upstairs.

Kara returned a short while later with a couple of carrier bags stuffed full of men's clothes and a very warm bright blue padded jacket.

"My ex left these behind, so if you don't mind that they are second hand, you are welcome to them," she said.

"Won't he want them back?" asked Jack astonished.

"No," Kara replied with a snort. "His new partner is much younger than me and he has a whole new trendy wardrobe now. Mutton dressed as Lamb, if you can say that about a man," she continued with a laugh.

"Are you sure?" asked Jack, as Kara handed him the bags.

"Yes, you'll be doing me a favour: they've been bagged up and in the way for ages, but I've just not got around to taking them to the charity shop."

That was true about the bags of clothes, but she didn't mention that she'd intended to eBay the jacket which had only been worn once on an ill-fated ski trip.

"The trousers will be much too big," she said, glancing at his thin frame, "so I've put an old belt in for you."

"Thank you so much," said Jack, "I don't know how I'll ever repay your kindness."

On impulse, he kissed her on the cheek and then left in a hurry, worried he'd overstepped the mark.

Kara closed the door and leaned against it for a moment, slightly flustered herself.

"Well, well, well," she said to herself. "I think a glass of wine is called for!"

Kara sat on the settee, the TV on low, slowly sipping her wine whilst letting her mind drift. The house creaked and settled around her, and for the first time since her husband left, she felt a little less alone.

# CHAPTER ELEVEN

Josie and Kara sat outside Josie's shed nursing mugs of tea and watched Jack work. He'd refused a cup himself, wanting to get straight on with digging.

"This is luxury," said Josie, "I could watch someone else work all day!"

"Me too," replied Kara, but Josie noticed with amusement that Kara's attention was more on the man than the work he was doing.

"Strange what you find in an allotment shed, isn't it?" continued Kara.

"Yes," said Josie with a hitch in her voice.

Kara turned to look at her and saw her stricken face, realising too late that Josie was thinking about the cats, not the man. Kara put her arms around Josie and gave her a long hug.

"Let me bring you up to date on the cats, Josie," she said when Josie had wiped her eyes and picked her mug up again.

"Please," said Josie, "I couldn't sleep for thinking about them."

"Well thanks to you, Ms Detective Josie, we have saved nine cats, three of whom are pregnant, the remaining six having given birth within the last few months. There are twenty-six kittens of varying ages. One of the cats is quite poorly, and all the cats and many of the kittens were undernourished, but we think they will all make it. They are a strong breed and should bounce back very quickly," explained Kara.

"Oh, thank goodness," exclaimed Josie, "I've been so worried, especially about the one that was so dehydrated."

"Well, she is the one who is still poorly, but you saved her life, Josie, and we think she will be just fine with a bit of TLC. It's unlikely she will ever be able to carry another litter, which makes her worthless for breeding, but she'll still be a great pet once recovered."

"I'll take her," said Josie, immediately, surprising herself. "That is, if her owner isn't found of course."

"Brilliant," said Kara with a grin, having hoped that Josie would offer. "Most of the cats are chipped, so their owners have already been informed, but that little one didn't have a chip, and neither did one other, so we haven't found their owners yet."

"I might be able to help you there, Kara," said Josie. I made up a document of all the cats that had been reported missing locally, by copying the 'Lost' posters, and each poster has a photo of the cat and a phone number or email for its owner."

"Wow, that's great, Josie. Can you email me it?" asked Kara.

"Sure. I'll go do that straight away, if you can look after Jack and lock my shed up before you go?" replied Josie.

"My pleasure," said Kara. She leaned back in her chair and happily resumed watching Jack work.

He was wearing a pair of her ex-husband's jeans, and although the belt was on its final hole, they still kept sliding down his hips a little, and he kept having to stop to hitch them up again. Despite that, Kara thought he looked far better in them than her ex ever did.

The blue ski jacket had been taken off as Jack got hot with digging and was hung carelessly on a fence post. Kara winced slightly, knowing how expensive it had been, and then laughed at herself: it had been hanging in the wardrobe unworn for three years – far better it was worn, even if that meant it got a bit grubby.

Kara's phone pinged with the emailed document from Josie and she quickly sent it onto her work colleagues and the local police. Sean had been arrested the previous afternoon and charged with stealing the cats and animal cruelty. At first, he had denied it all, but when confronted with the evidence, he admitted both charges and was later released on bail pending prosecution.

Kara knew that, as there was a high level of culpability and harm caused, Sean would get a very large fine, and, she prayed, a custodial sentence too. Despite working for the RSPCA part time for many years, she was still shocked and saddened by people's cruelty, and without her realising it, a lone tear rolled down her cheek. A hand on her shoulder brought her back to the present, and she looked up to see Jack looking at her with concern.

"You okay, Kara?" he asked gently.
"I will be," she said with a shaky laugh. "Are you okay?"
"I will be," he replied.

# CHAPTER TWELVE

Kara hadn't been able to stay long with him at the allotments as it was her day for helping at the food bank, followed by picking up her children from school. As soon as she'd gone, Jack missed her cheerful chatter and warm smile. He kept on working until the soil was perfect, then cleaned the tools, locked them in the shed and returned the key to Josie. He was touched that Kara had trusted him to lock up Josie's shed… after all, he had broken into hers and stolen people's vegetables!

Josie didn't seem surprised to see him and asked him in for a cup of tea, which he was very happy to accept. Her cottage was warm and welcoming and he soon relaxed into the squishy settee and was nearly asleep when she returned with a tray of tea and biscuits. Jack wasn't a bit surprised when Josie told him she used to be a Headmistress: she had that air of quiet authority and kindness about her. Before long, under her gentle questioning, he found himself opening up about his previous life.

"Sounds like you had a breakdown, Jack," she said quietly.

"I think you're right," he said sadly. "My brain just shut down, and well, I guess it was easier existing in a non-life rather than facing up to things."

"And do you think you are ready to move on now?"

"Yes. Yes, I do. Something about Kirkby, the allotments, the people, makes me feel that I can do it," he said. "I feel like I can breathe here."

"What did you use to do?" asked Josie.

"I was an accountant and worked in an office all day. I hated it, and to make it worse, I did bookkeeping in the evenings to earn extra money" Jack replied.

"Why accountancy?" asked Josie?

"I don't know really. I was good at maths at school, and a job came up which offered training and good money just as we were about to get married, so it seemed the sensible thing to do," he said, shaking his head at the memory.

"What would you like to do?" asked Josie.

"I'd like to work outside as much as I can. I'd like to be self-employed, if that was possible, so gardener/handyman would be good, if I could learn more about gardening," he said, looking at her with a slight question on his face.

Josie nodded, knowing that he would easily pick up bits of gardening work and that she had plenty of time to teach him the basics.

Jack paused and thought for a moment.

"I'd also like to work with children. I really enjoyed being with Lily and Ronan yesterday."

Josie's eyebrows shot up. Kara hadn't told her that Jack had met her children. That was a special privilege as she was very protective of them and rarely took anyone home. She must trust him, and Josie realised she did too, and was prepared to take a chance on him.

"Well, the school's been advertising for a part-time trainee teaching assistant. I can put a word in for you..." Josie said.

"That would be wonderful!" exclaimed Jack. "Thank you so much!"

"You might not thank me when you have Year 3's running you ragged," she said with a smile.

Josie told him what being a teaching assistant would involve, and then it was her turn to open up as she told him about the awful events of the previous day. Jack was a good listener, and Josie felt better for talking about it.

Eventually Jack got up to go, realising it had grown dark outside. Josie insisted on paying him £50 for digging over her allotment, despite his protestations that it was too much; she had laughed and said saving her aching back was worth considerably more!

Jack was now in the unusual position of actually having some money in his pocket. The church outreach programme was covering his rent until his benefits came in, and another allotment holder, Ben, had asked if he could dig his plot over too, so he had work for the next day as well.

Jack walked through the town to his lodgings past the honey-coloured stone of the old houses warmly lit by streetlights. People smiled, nodded or muttered 'Evening' as he passed, and Jack felt a sense of belonging. A wonderful smell of fish and chips drew him to the chip shop and he treated himself to a portion of chips but decided against a fish as well as he needed to make his money last. They were hot and crispy, which was wonderful on a cold evening, but he found himself remembering yesterday's burnt sausage and oven chips, and somehow, tonight's supper didn't compare.

# CHAPTER THIRTEEN

Benjamin and Zoe had moved to Kirkby from London the previous year. Benjamin, or Ben as his friends called him, was an IT security specialist and Zoe a website designer. Sick of the London rat race and knowing that they could work from home easily enough, they had sold their tiny flat and moved 'up north'.

They had a dream of being self-sufficient, growing their own veg and maybe having a few chickens and a goat. Zoe had done her research and found that the allotments in Kirkby were well regarded, so she had put their name down for one well over a year ago. Their names reached the top of the waiting list almost at the same time as their eventual house move the previous autumn, the sale and purchase having been a long, drawn out process.

With things to do on the house, Christmas and then the winter weather, their first visit to their new allotment had been yesterday. They had stood, hand in hand, looking at the stony soil, the row of something more brown than green and the semi-derelict shed, and had no idea where to start. They watched Jack diligently digging manure into a neighbouring plot and thought that preparing the soil was probably the best way to start. It looked very hard work though, and when Jack stopped for a breather and they got chatting, they quickly asked him if he would do it for them.

When he agreed, Zoe had been relieved, knowing that she could spend the time designing the planting on her computer instead. Ben had also been happy at the prospect of a drive through the wonderful Yorkshire countryside with the valid excuse of visiting a large garden centre in York to buy tools and a new shed.

As he dug, Jack smiled to himself thinking of Ben and Zoe. They were a striking couple; her, slim with masses of red hair and very pale skin due her Scottish roots, and him, broad shouldered and dark skinned due to his families' Caribbean heritage. They were so in love with each other and with their new life and their energy and shared enthusiasm was infectious.

Jack realised that he and Julie hadn't had any shared passions, apart from for each other and that had waned slowly without them realising it. He stopped digging for a moment and leaned on the spade, taking in the view over the town and hills behind and taking in deep breaths of crisp, clean air.

A robin landed on the soil in front of him, its red chest vivid against the dark soil. It had a brief tussle pulling a large worm from the rich earth and then flew off to enjoy its meal in a nearby tree. Moments later its high-pitched trembling song filled the air, and when Jack listened carefully, he could hear in the gaps between runs the response of another robin.

It seemed everyone had a partner, and he wondered if he would ever be part of a couple again. He knew if he was blessed with a second chance, he would cherish every moment, making time for each other every day, having fun, doing stuff together, not waiting for some mystical time in the future when they had enough money. He had lived for months with nothing at all, and now that he had a roof over his head and just a little money, he felt like a millionaire.

His thoughts strayed to Kara who had been so kind to him, but much as he really liked her, he thought she had enough on her plate with her recent divorce and the children and wouldn't want him coming on to her. Besides, what did he have to offer? He was technically still married and an unemployed homeless bum with, if he was honest, mental health problems. He had run away from home after all! Maybe if he was able to secure the teaching assistant post he'd be a bit more respectable and then maybe, just maybe, he could ask her out.

Josie had got him the application forms, so Jack decided he'd call on her on his way home and ask her to help him complete them. With her inside knowledge, she'd be able to steer him towards the right tone that would, hopefully, get him an interview at least.

Job finished, tools cleaned and put away, Jack made his way down the hill feeling more at peace with himself and the world than he had for a long time. The sun was just setting in a last-minute blaze, turning the stone walls of the houses that welcomed him to rose, the red clouds above a promise of a good day tomorrow.

# CHAPTER FOURTEEN

Going through the application forms with Josie the previous evening they had soon realised that Jack would need some identification, some proof of who he was for the DBS checks at the very least. So now he was on a bus, heading for Leeds, feeling very strange to be returning to his hometown. It was only about eight months since he'd left home, but it felt like a whole lifetime ago. The bus pulled into the bus station, and although he had lived here for most of his life, stepping out into the bustling city felt like stepping into a foreign land.

Rather than take another bus, Jack decided to walk, partly because walking calmed him, but mainly to delay having to face Julie. The flat was on the fourth floor, and when Jack arrived at the familiar front door his heart was hammering in his chest, partly from the stairs and partly with nerves. The door was opened by a complete stranger, and for a moment Jack felt relief, but then frustration as he still needed to find Julie.

Fortunately, she had left a forwarding address, and Jack soon found himself walking along a nice tree-lined street and then up a drive to a smart detached house. He wondered if he'd been given the wrong address, but the door opened before he reached it and standing there was Julie. A very pregnant Julie.

"You're alive then," she said.

"You're pregnant then," he said, realising that he was stating the obvious, but he was finding it difficult to take in. "Is it mine?" he asked, looking into her eyes for the first time.

"No Jack, it's not yours. Sorry; I know you always wanted children," said Julie gently. "Come in Jack, we need to talk."

A couple of hours later Jack left, taking nothing from his marriage but a carrier bag full of documents. There had been no recriminations, just explanations on both sides, talking calmly like old friends rather than old lovers. They both realised that they had outgrown each other long before Julie's affair with a doctor at the hospital where she worked.

Rather than be cross, Jack found he was relieved that Julie had found someone she was obviously deeply in love with, and he genuinely wished her all the best. They agreed to get a divorce as soon as possible, and as Jack walked back to the bus station, he felt like a weight had been lifted off his shoulders.

# CHAPTER FIFTEEN

Josie had taken a call from the police just as she was about to get into the bath. They were just informing her that they wouldn't need to return to the building on Sean's allotment plot and it could be cleaned up. Josie shivered at the thought of that unpleasant task, and at the cold draught in her bathroom. She had just put one foot into her bath when the phone rang again. Knowing the answering machine would pick it up, Josie sunk into the warm water and continued her morning ablutions.

Whoever was calling was impatient, as it was only five minutes later when the phone rang again and then again just a few moments later. With a sigh, Josie stepped out of her bath, wrapped a towel around herself and grabbed the phone just as the person on the other end hung up. Josie decided to get dressed before checking for any message, but as she rubbed herself dry, the phone rang yet again.

"Is that Ms Greenwood?" said a booming male voice.

"Yes," she replied curtly. "And you are?"

"Councillor Smythe," he replied.

Josie racked her brains but couldn't recollect having ever spoken to him before.

"And how can I help you, Councillor?" she asked.

"Well, you can start by answering your phone promptly in future," he said. "When I leave a message, I expect to be called straight back!"

Josie was incensed but fought to stay calm.

"I'm sorry, but who are you?" she asked.

"Who am I? You mean you don't know? I am a former Lord Mayor and the Chair of the Parks and Open Spaces Committee at the Council!" he said pompously.

"What happened to Councillor Andrews?" Josie asked, unaware that lovely Councillor Andrews, who had held that position for years, had stepped down.

"I expect to be informed immediately when there has been a serious breach of the Allotment Rules!" Councillor Smythe continued, rudely ignoring her question.

"To what are you referring?" asked Josie, frostily.

"I'm referring to your dereliction of duty by allowing an illegal business to take place on the allotments. Your action has brought great embarrassment on the Council," he said.

"My action! I've not done anything!" spluttered Josie.

"Precisely Ms Greenwood. You didn't do anything to stop it, and you failed to inform me of your failing," said the Councillor smugly.

"It's *Mrs* Greenwood," she said crossly, "and I think you need to find out the facts before you make accusations."

"How dare you speak to me like that! I am a former Lord Mayor and deserve respect," he exploded.

"Yes, and I am a former Headmistress, and I won't be spoken to like a naughty five-year-old. Good day to you Councillor," replied Josie, hanging up the phone without waiting for his response.

Josie realised she was shaking, partly from cold as she was still wrapped in the damp towel, and partly from indignation. What an obnoxious man! As chair of the Allotment Association Josie would be producing a report to be circulated to allotment holders and the Council at the AGM in March, but there was no requirement that she knew of (and having been Chair for over twenty years, she knew the rules well) to make interim reports to the Council. Regardless, she had thought it insensitive to make public any details of the cat business until all the cats had been reunited with their owners.

Thinking of that, she wondered how 'her' little cat was doing and decided to ring Kara up for an update. Once Kara had reassured her that the cat was doing well, but was still unclaimed, Josie relayed the conversation with Councillor Smythe. Kara was incensed but howled with laughter at Josie's impression of the self-important man and Josie's put down, leaving Josie feeling a bit better.

She was belatedly making her breakfast when there was a knock at the door; it was going to be one of those days. However, it was only Jack bringing his ID, and curious about how his meeting with his wife had gone the previous day, Josie asked him to join her for breakfast. Jack was delighted, not having eaten since a bland sandwich in the bus station the day before. Instead of just cereal and toast, Josie found herself frying up bacon and eggs whilst Jack made tea and toast.

Whilst they tucked into what was now brunch, Jack told Josie about his trip to Leeds, his pregnant soon-to-be-ex-wife, and his relief on getting 'home' to Kirkby. Josie told him about her phone calls that morning and Jack was furious at the way the Councillor had spoken to her. She also mentioned, with a shudder, that she would need to clean out the shed where the cats had been imprisoned. When Jack put his hand over hers and told her he would do it, she was too relieved to protest.

# CHAPTER SIXTEEN

The smell in the barn was awful and Jack flung the doors open wide to let in some fresh air. The little kitten bodies were already decomposing and covered in flies, which flew into his face as he approached. Jack pulled his t-shirt up over his nose, regretting now that he had had a cooked breakfast with Josie as it was threatening to reappear. However, he was glad it was him, not Josie, having to deal with it, especially as it gave him a small way to repay her kindness.

He decided to dig a grave first to allow time for some of the smell and flies to disperse and selected a spot on the very edge of the plot which was lit with dappled sunlight through the bare tree branches. He dug deep to stop the grave being disturbed by any planting on the allotment, and after covering the bodies over and tamping the soil down, he spent time fashioning a cross from bits of fallen twigs.

Jack felt he should say something, but no words came to him, so he just bowed his head in quiet contemplation for a moment. The thought came to him that he could have been found dead from hypothermia in Kara's shed just a few weeks ago and he wondered if anyone would have stood at his graveside and mourned him.

Shaking off the morbid thought, Jack set to clearing out the barn, repeatedly filling a bucket and swilling the floor with disinfectant till the space smelt clean. He closed the doors and stood with his back to them looking down the hill across the allotments. A pale sun was just coming out, lighting the edges of plants and buildings, glowing through greenhouse glass and making the view look like an oil painting by an old master. He could see a few people working on their plots and he liked the sense of industry and the feeling of being part of a continuity of self-sufficiency.

Jack looked around the plot he was standing on, and the neighbouring plot, both of which were a tangle of weeds, and itched to get stuck in and make them orderly like the other plots. Josie had told him that she had found out that Sean's wife had held the neighbouring plot under her maiden name, presumably to keep people away from the barn.

Due to the pre-existing structure of the barn, Sean's plot was bigger than most, and with the barn to keep gardening equipment in, plus the direct access through the woods, it would make a great base to establish a small gardening business. Jack felt a fizz of excitement at the prospect and decided to ask Josie to put his name down. Although he knew there was a waiting list, he recollected that she had said that the soil was poor here, and that people preferred the plots lower down, if possible, so he may be in with a chance.

Jack knelt down to take a handful of soil from the spoil heap left from digging the grave. It certainly was very claggy, with chunks of orange clay running through it, but if he could dig in leaf mould from the adjacent woods and as much horse manure as was available he'd soon get it into a better condition. The weak sunlight glinted off something small caught in a solid lump of clay: the only visible part of it was shiny and Jack picked it up to examine it. Whatever it was, was caught fast in the clay so Jack wrapped it in a tissue and dropped it into his pocket to clean up and have a look at later.

On his way back to the B&B, Jack called at Josie's to ask her to put his name down for an allotment plot. Josie was happy to add him to the list; she thought he should be able to get that specific plot and perhaps the one next to it too, as they were not ones they had expected to become available. Josie also had some good news for him: he had an interview the following week for the teaching assistant position at the school. He would need to drop in proof of identity and qualifications as soon as possible, so Jack dashed straight home to sort through the bag of papers he had brought back from Leeds.

Jack soon found his birth certificate, his school GCSE and A Level certificates and his accountancy qualifications. References were going to be a problem – he'd just disappeared without giving any notice, so a glowing reference was unlikely. Jack thought the quickest thing to do was to ring them up, which would mean borrowing Joyce, his landlady's, phone again. She didn't seem to mind, and Jack was soon through to his old boss, Jonathan.

"Jack, Jack Brown?" said Jonathan. "Wow, it's good to hear from you, Jack – we thought you were dead or abducted by aliens!"

"I'm so sorry, Jonathan. I think I had a breakdown. Something happened that I don't want to go into, and I've just been, well, lost for months. But now I'm back!"

"I'm sorry Jack, you can't come back – I've filled your post," said Jonathan, misunderstanding him.

"I'm sure they can't be as good as me," said Jack, with a laugh, "but don't worry, that's not why I'm ringing."

"Oh, what can I do for you?"

"Well, I know it's very cheeky in the circumstances, but any chance I can have a reference?" asked Jack, crossing his fingers.

"No problem Jack. Until you went AWOL, you were a conscientious worker and you are right," he said, lowering his voice, "the new guy is nowhere near as good!"

Jack thanked him and then gave him the school's address to send the reference. After a few more minutes of chatting, catching up about colleagues, Jack rang off after Jonathan had wished him all the best in his new career. Jack returned the phone to Joyce and went back to sorting through his papers. He came across a pile of bank statements and realised there was quite a lot of money in his savings account, money he'd been saving to buy a family house.

Julie had had her own savings account, and they'd had a joint account for rent, bills, food etc. so this money was his. After months of living with no money at all, it seemed like a fortune. Jack felt a flare of hope in his chest: maybe, just maybe, once he had an income of his own again, he might be able to put down a deposit on a flat or house in Kirkby. Properties were less expensive here than in Leeds, and Jack found himself fantasying about a small 'roses around the door' cottage like Josie's, and the possibility of inviting Kara round for a meal one day.

Borrowing Joyce's phone again, with a promise to get his own as soon as he could, he rang the bank to see what he needed to do to get access to his accounts again. He was shocked to find his accounts had been frozen in his prolonged absence. To unlock it he'd have to go into a branch with a photo driving license, a utility bill or some other proof of identify and address, and a wage slip with his NI number on it. The dream of his own small place faded as he realised it wasn't going to happen anytime soon.

# CHAPTER SEVENTEEN

Lady Dorothy Kirkby gazed out of her window at the pale sunshine gilding the allotments. Dazzled by the sun, for a moment she saw instead the formal gardens of her youth, the smooth lawns, the neatly laid out paths and clipped yew hedges, the rose garden and the kitchen garden. She blinked, and the view resolved back into the present. The only thing that remained the same was the carriage house at the edge of the woods.

There had been a lot of comings and goings there recently, including police and RSPCA officers, which she'd watched with interest. Apart from the carer who came in every morning and evening, she saw no one all day and enjoyed the excitement, but felt guilty for doing so when later she read about the cat breeding scandal in the papers.

Now today there was this man at the carriage house who reminded her so much of her beloved Henry. Although this man's hair was far too long, tied back in a ridiculous ponytail, his height and slim frame and the way he carried himself was so like Henry's that Dorothy felt a tear run down her cheek. The very last time she had seen Henry had been in that barn, the evening before he returned to his regiment.

He left her with an engagement ring and the beginning of a new life. Within a year, she had lost him, the baby and the ring.

Just a few years after that tragedy she was hit again, this time with the death of her parents. Her father died of pneumonia after catching flu the year following the end of the war, his lungs having never fully recovered from being gassed in the trenches in the first world war. Her mother, who suffered from bouts of depression and who had always enjoyed drinking a little more than she ought to at social occasions, took to drinking on her own and died of liver failure just eighteen months after her husband's death. Dorothy liked to think her mother drank because she missed her husband so much, but if she was honest, they had never been a particularly close couple, and her mother's drinking was more to blot out whatever blackness she had in her head.

Dorothy fought hard not to fall into a black hole of her own but living alone in the manor was hard and lonely. It was far too big for one person, and as no one could ever replace her beloved Henry and her dead child, she had no intention of ever marrying. She used some of the money she had inherited to convert the manor into luxury apartments, retaining a three-bedroom ground floor apartment for herself. The rent from the other apartments more than covered her monthly outgoings, so she was financially secure and could remain independent.

Most of the grounds had been dug up to grow vegetables during the war, and Dorothy, having been a Land Girl herself, liked the idea of that usage continuing and gave them to the Council to be used as allotments, on the proviso that the carriage house barn remained.

Dorothy looked around her elegant sitting room with its high ceilings and wood panelling. This had been the morning room and she had always liked it, but the main reason that she had insisted that this room was part of her apartment was for the view over the valley. A view not only of the rising and setting sun each day, but of the carriage house where she had once known love.

# CHAPTER EIGHTEEN

It had been a while since Kara had seen Jack, and she didn't know if he was avoiding her or had just been busy. To be fair, she'd been busy too with the kids being home over half term. She'd had a week off work to be with them, but it had been hard work keeping them entertained due to the weather still being cold and there not being many places open until Easter. Normally Andy had them for part of each holiday, but he'd gone off skiing with his new wife – a sort of 'late honeymoon' he'd said as an excuse not to take the kids with him.

They were back at school today, and she heaved a sigh of relief: much as she adored them, looking after them for a full week on her own was hard work. Dashing round the local shops to replenish her diminished food stocks, she had got chatting with Joyce whilst waiting to be served in the bakers. Joyce was lovely, but did like to gossip, so Kara soon knew exactly how many times Jack had borrowed her phone and who he'd rung.

Kara hadn't given the fact Jack didn't have a phone a moment's thought; she couldn't imagine how anyone managed nowadays without one. She remembered that she had an old pay-as-you-go phone at home that didn't do much more than make calls. She'd been keeping it to give Ronan as his first phone; he nagged her regularly for one, but she still thought he was too young. Having put the shopping away, she delved through her 'all-sorts' drawer until she found it, put it onto charge and then went online and to top up the credit on it. She'd learnt from Joyce that Jack had a job interview, so he could pay her back once he was gainfully employed.

"Ta-da!" said Kara, brandishing her old phone in the air when Jack answered her knock.

"Kara! How lovely to see you," said Jack with a warm smile, "but how…"

"Did I know you needed a phone?" finished Kara, stepping into the room and closing the door behind her.

Jack stepped back, a bit surprised, whilst casting a furtive look around his room. Thankfully, he'd made the bed this morning and the upside of having so few possessions was that the room looked reasonably tidy. However, having Kara and a bed in close proximity was doing things to his blood pressure, so he stepped over to the window and opened it a little, hoping that the cold air would take the sudden flush from his face.

"If you want all of Kirkby to know what you are doing, tell Joyce," said Kara in a stage whisper.

"Ah!" said Jack with a grin, taking the phone from her outstretched hand. "Are you sure?" he asked, nodding at the phone. "You are so kind!"

"My pleasure," she said, grinning back.

She looked lovely when she smiled and Jack found he was heating up again. He needed to get her out of this room before he did something that might spoil their friendship.

"Well, I can't pay you back just yet, but I can just about manage a coffee, if you have time?" he asked picking up his jacket.

"I have all the time in the world to waste today," Kara replied with a happy sigh, "but if you'd seen me last week trying to entertain the kids all week, I wouldn't have time to even say 'Hello'!"

"Oh, you should have given me a shout," said Jack as they walked up the street toward the Cosy Café. "It would have been good practice for my job, should I get it." He gave her a sideways look. "I suppose you know all about that too?"

"Yep!" she replied with a laugh. "I also know that you haven't anything suitable to wear for an interview."

"How do you know that?" asked Jack, puzzled. "I'm sure I never mentioned it to Joyce."

"Well, unless you have been on a shopping spree, all you have is my ex-husbands old clothes, and, lovely as you look in that blue jacket, it won't work for a job interview."

Jack glanced down at the jacket and knew she was right. A bright blue padded jacket with mud smears on it didn't say 'suitable to work at a school'. Jack's face fell, the joy of being with Kara washed away by worrying about how he could possibly afford new clothes.

"Don't worry Jack, I have a plan. I'm gasping for a coffee and then afterwards we'll get you sorted. Don't worry, it will be in budget!"

Jack didn't have a budget and did worry. A couple of coffees was the extent of what he could manage at present, ironic when he knew he had thousands in a savings account he couldn't access. However, his luck was in, as Ben and Zoe were enjoying a coffee and cake in the café and Ben came straight over and paid him the £50 he owed him for digging over his allotment. Jack introduced Kara to the couple and then went to order the coffees, adding on impulse a large slice of chocolate cake for Kara now he had some more funds.

"Better than sex!" announced Kara, savouring a large mouthful of cake and Jack found himself getting hot again.

"So glad I've seen you, Jack," said Ben. "We didn't know where to find you – we didn't have a mobile number and couldn't see you online, apart from someone of the same name that looked a bit like you at an accountants' firm in Leeds."

"Well, I didn't have a mobile, until a few moments ago, and I don't have a website, I'm afraid," said Jack.

"How on earth do you run your business?" asked Zoe.

"My business?" queried Jack.

"Yeah, you know, gardening etcetera," replied Ben. "We were just fortifying ourselves with cake before trying to build the shed that's been delivered in bits this morning, but, mate, it would be so much easier with your help!"

"Happy to help," said Jack, "but as a friend; you've paid me enough for the digging already."

"Tell you what Jack," said Zoe, if I can leave you boys to play with bits of wood all afternoon, I'd be more than happy to build you a nice little website instead as payment. That way us, and others, can find you when we need you!"

Jack stared at her open-mouthed. "That would be brilliant Zoe!"

He looked around the little group gathered around the café table with its cheery red gingham cloth and felt a warm glow inside: he had friends!

Ben and Zoe left to check the shed delivery, inviting Jack and Kara for dinner at the weekend before they went. Before he could protest that they weren't a couple, Kara accepted for both of them, as long as she could get Josie to babysit. The warm glow inside Jack intensified as he watched Kara lick her cake-sticky fingers. He'd forgotten to get her a napkin, so he reached into his pocket, hoping for a clean tissue, but his hand came out with a tissue covered lump of crumbly mud instead.

"Yuck, what on earth have you got in your pocket, Jack?" asked Kara.

"I'm not sure – I forgot all about it," said Jack as he gently prised the now dry mud apart.

Kara pushed her crumb-laden plate underneath to catch the falling soil, and then gasped in astonishment as the clump parted to reveal a magnificent ring. The rich yellow gold gleamed as good as new, but the stones in the ring were still encrusted with mud. Janet, the café owner, having heard their gasps of astonishment came to have a look and quickly brought a cup of hot water over.

They all watched in silence as the mud dissolved and the gemstones were revealed. Set in the centre was the largest diamond they had ever seen, with a half-moon of sapphires on either side and an oval of diamonds surrounding it all. They were mounted in white gold, silver or maybe platinum, with stylised flowers delicately cut into the underside of the mount and shoulders of the ring.

"Wow!" they all said, almost in unison.

"Where did you find it Jack?" asked Kara, staring at the stunning ring in astonishment.

"On the allotment," replied Jack, almost unable to speak.

Janet then fetched a clean cup of water and a tea towel, and having given it another rinse, buffed up the ring and held it up to the light. It sparkled brightly, sending rainbows of light across the room as she turned it to exam it.

"Looks like art deco to me," said Janet, handing it back to an astonished Jack. "Late period probably, but I'd need to check. You're one lucky man – if its real, it will be worth a fortune!"

"How do you know?" asked Kara, taking the ring from Jack, slipping it onto her third finger right hand and turning her hand this way and that to catch the light.

"My dad has the Antiques Shop in the High Street," said Janet. "I've grown up around vintage jewellery and this period is my favourite. I could get dad to value it for you if you want?"

"Shouldn't I just hand it into the police?" asked Jack.

"Well yes, I suppose so," said Janet, "but it would be good to check it's not just brass and paste first, so that you are not wasting their time."

That agreed, Kara reluctantly removed the ring and handed it to Janet, before Jack paid for their coffees and they stepped out, slightly shell-shocked, into the street again.

Jack followed Kara into the charity shop a few doors up in a bit of a dream, not just at the stunning ring he'd found, but seeing it on Kara's hand. There was a faint white line on her finger that he'd noticed for the first time, evidence that once she had been loved and cherished, as the owner of the ring had once been. He had an urge to be the one to cherish her, but then he remembered that he must have felt the same about Julie once and she had cheated on him, so was he ready to open his heart up to possible hurt again?

"Here," said Kara, nudging him before handing him a large pile of men's trousers and shirts. "You were miles away! Just in case you've not just become rich, we need to get you organised for your interview. Changing room over there," she said pointing to a flimsy looking curtain in the corner of the shop.

To Jack's embarrassment, the curtain only came to mid-thigh and billowed away from the sides every time anyone walked past. Not only that, but he knew his only pair of socks were full of holes and not fit to be on display to the good people of Kirkby. Thankfully, he was pretty sure his baggy, faded underpants where at least hidden from view. Kara seemed to be enjoying his discomfort, however, passing comment on his white muscular legs and laughing every time the curtain moved.

Despite that, Jack found a pair of black trousers that fitted him reasonably well and were only a bit too long. The price tag was £3, so he knew he could manage that okay. Two shirts more or less fitted him, a pale grey one, and a light blue one that he liked best but that was slightly frayed around the cuffs. Kara narrowed her eyes and squinted at him when he showed her each one, and then confirmed that the blue one suited him best.

"You won't see the cuffs under a jacket," she said, and then proceeded to hand him jacket after jacket to try on before she finally declared that a dark grey jacket was perfect.

The jacket was £5 and the shirt £2, so for £10 he had his interview wardrobe. Kara had an armful of children's clothes she'd picked out, so he handed her £10 to pay for his at the same time as her own shopping whilst he put his boots back on. A pair of shoes would have been good too, but if he polished up the old boots, he hoped they wouldn't look too bad. Kara returned and handed him two carrier bags.

"She put in some socks to make up for the frayed cuffs," she said nonchalantly as they left the shop.

Jack had the suspicion that that wasn't true, and that Kara had bought them for him, but he said nothing, resolving to spoil her in return as soon as he had some regular money coming in. They then parted company, Jake to take his new clothes home before going to join Ben at the allotment, and Kara to start getting the kid's lunch ready. Without thinking, Jack instinctively leaned in to kiss her cheek as a goodbye, wishing he didn't have his hands full of shopping bags and that maybe he could have held her close for a moment too.

# CHAPTER NINETEEN

Jack was enjoying working alongside Ben erecting the shed. The weather was mild, and although the instructions weren't the best they had made steady progress. The work took his mind off the news he had received earlier that morning that Julie had had her baby, a little girl. Despite the way their relationship had ended, he was happy for her, but sad that he was unlikely to have a family of his own.

Zoe turned up with cans of Coke for them, and started snapping photos of them on her phone whilst they worked.

"For your website, Jack. Either that, or for a porn site!" she said with a laugh.

Once the shed was up, Ben went to buy some deep green paint, a colour specified in the Allotment Rules. Whilst he waited, Jack decided he would weed and tidy up the paths that ran through the allotments. He wasn't sure if someone was employed to look after the common areas or if each allotment holder just did their bit, but he was happy to help.

Over the next couple of days Jack returned and continued tidying the paths and common areas. As he worked, he chatted to the few allotment holders who were working on their plots, sharing mugs of tea and getting to know the community. In doing so, he picked up a couple of other bits of work, which meant he had a trickle of money coming in.

By the end of the second day, he couldn't wait any longer and called into the Cosy Café to see if Janet had any news about the ring.

"Hi Jack," said Janet, "I'm pleased you've popped in. Dad just rang: can you go and see him at the shop?"

"Yes, thanks Janet. Fingers crossed!" he replied.

The Antiques Shop was in one of the oldest shops in town, with low ceilings and even lower oak beams that meant you had to watch your head as you wandered through the maze of treasures. A sprightly elderly man with a shock of white hair suddenly materialised from the back somewhere and beckoned

Jack up to the counter. He introduced himself as Gerrard, and when Jack told him who he was he shook his hand warmly.

Unlocking a drawer, Gerrard drew out the ring and placed it on a blue velvet cushion where strategically placed lights made it sparkle and shine. It had obviously had a professional clean and looked brand new.

"Well Jack, I've got some good news and some bad news for you," said Gerrard.

Jack looked at him expectantly and waited.

"The good news is that it's all genuine. The centre diamond is 6.6 carats, old European cut and about as flawless as you can get, with about another seven carats in total in the diamonds around the sides. Velvety blue Sri Lankan sapphires, an art deco platinum mount and an 18-carat gold band. Date and maker's mark tell me it was made by Cartier in 1939. I'm awaiting a few calls back on value, but on what I've heard back so far, you are looking at around £70,000 – £90,000."

Gerrard paused and drew a breath at last, looking Jack steadily in the eye.

Jack gulped but struggling to speak.

"And the bad news?" he finally croaked out.

"I'm pretty sure I should be able to find out who it belonged to," said Gerrard.

Jack stared at him. He didn't know whether to be upset or relieved.

"See here," said Gerrard, passing him his eye glass and pointing to what Jack had taken to be scratches on the inside on the ring band. "This inscription."

Jack squinted through the lens until tiny writing swam into focus.

"My one and only love" it said.

"Although it was made by one of the world's best jewellers, there is only one man I know of that could have done so tiny an inscription and he lived in Yorkshire," said Gerrard.

"Who," asked Jack, distracted by a strong wave of emotion upon seeing the inscription.

"My father," said Gerrard.

Gerrard went on to explain that if his late father had done the inscription, as he strongly believed, there would be a record of it. Apparently, his father never threw anything away, however, his old records were in storage in the loft, and not stored in any kind of order, so it could be a very long time before a record of who commissioned the inscription could be discovered.

They agreed that Jack would leave the ring with Gerrard and that he would inform the police of the discovery and the efforts being made to find the owner. Jack snapped a few photos of the ring, thanked Gerrard warmly and then left the shop in a bit of a daze.

He'd forgotten that he and Kara were going to Ben and Zoe's that evening until she knocked on the door, startling him. They were going in her car as the couple lived in a tiny village about 15 minutes' drive away. It felt strangely intimate being in a car with Kara, especially as it was dark outside already, cocooning them in the small warm space.

Satnav took them to the address, and they were both surprised that it was a tiny stone cottage in a row of old cottages in a village of just one street, an ancient church and a pub.

"I thought that, coming from London, they'd have a palatial detached house," said Kara as they waited on the doorstep.

Jack nodded in agreement, but when Ben opened the door, they could immediately see why the couple had bought the house. Inside, two or three cottages had been knocked together, giving a vast open space. There were large settees piled with colourful cushions at one end in front of a roaring log burner and a modern white kitchen with a huge white island unit at the other. Apart from a complete wall of floor to ceiling glass, all the walls were white and hung with large abstract canvases in vibrant colours.

"Wow," said Jack and Kara in unison.

"I can see why you bought this house, Ben, it's stunning!" said Kara, looking around in wonder.

"We love it," said Zoe, coming out from behind the island to kiss them both, "but the main reason we bought it is this."

Zoe flicked a switch and floodlights came on outside the wall of glass illuminating the view. There was virtually no garden, just a small, paved seating area boarded by a low dry-stone wall, but the landscape rose behind it up a gentle hill to a magnificent tree standing alone on the horizon. Its bare branches were silhouetted against the moon, but Jake could imagine how wonderful it would look in full leaf.

"It's strange," said Ben, "we wanted a vast garden vegetables and chickens, but settled for a yard with a view of a tree."

"I can understand that," said Jack, taking a swig of the beer that Zoe had just put in his hand. "There's something about the timelessness of this view that is powerful yet calming. I could happily look at it all day!"

"That's just it, Jack. I'm glad you feel it too," said Ben, smiling at him.

"Well, you can't stand and look at it all this evening," said Zoe, flicking off the floodlights. "Dinner's ready."

They followed her into a small intimate dining room set off to one side of the main open space. All four walls were painted the deepest indigo, but the room was lit with turquoise glass lamps and the table was full of candles, so it wasn't dark. The colour reminded Jack of the sapphires in the ring, and whilst they tucked into a delicious fragrant curry he updated Kara on the information that Gerrard had given him. Ben and Zoe were unaware of the find, so Jack filled them in and showed them the pictures on his phone.

"Nice as it would be to be able to keep the ring, I'd much rather find the person who'd lost it," said Jack.

"If you don't want it, I'd be very happy to take it off your hands, Jack," joked Kara.

"If we don't find who owns it and I'm allowed to keep it, I'll give it to you," replied Jack, remembering how it had fit perfectly on her finger.

"Right, yes, as if!" she replied, laughing.

"She's got witnesses, Jack," laughed Zoe, but Jack just smiled and said nothing.

They had a lovely, relaxed evening chatting easily about everything and nothing, and they were both sad to leave, but Kara had to get back to pick up the children from Josie's. Kara promised to return the invitation soon and Jack added a similar invite to his mental list for when he had his own place.

Back at Josie's, Jack carried the sleepy children to the car, and then, his hands free, pulled Kara into a quick hug before she too got into the car and drove home. Josie, seeing the sad look on his face as Kara's car disappeared, and knowing that returning to his small room at the B&B might seem hard after an evening of company, invited him in for a nightcap.

Josie's little cat, Lucky, climbed onto his lap, turned round a few times and then went to sleep, its warmth and gentle snores relaxing him and making him smile.

Over a small brandy, Jack told her all about the ring and showed her the pictures on his phone, explaining that it might take a while to find out who had bought it.

"Actually Jack, it's not who bought it that matters really," said Josie, "but who he gave it to!"

"You're right," said Jack, nodding. "That's who we need to find."

"Well, the person who bought it must have been someone with a lot of money," ruminated Kara, "and, given the times, the recipient is likely to have been well off, in the same social class."

"Good thinking. Hopefully, that narrows it down a bit?" replied Jack.

"Leave it with me Jack: I like a good mystery," said Josie.

# SPRING

# CHAPTER TWENTY

It was a lovely spring morning and Josie walked through the allotments with joy in her heart – she loved this time of year. The daffodils that had been tight green buds were now fully out, a glorious golden ribbon laced through the allotments. Their heavy heads nodded in greeting as Josie passed and she stopped to enjoy their cheer and note the new growth greening the allotments all around her. She also noticed how neat and tidy all the paths between allotments were and wondered who had been hard at work: she had a sneaking suspicion it was Jack, but he hadn't mentioned it.

Josie paused as she passed Hugo's plot and admired his neat rows of seedlings and raised mounds where she knew potatoes would be nestled. She still hadn't met the man and felt bad, as, being the Chair of the Allotment Association, she usually went out of her way to welcome all new allotment holders personally. She liked to gently explain the rules, rather than just email or post them, as that was less officious, but so far she hadn't done either for Hugo. However, looking at his plot, it didn't look like he needed reminding of the rules, he was obviously a thoughtful and careful gardener, unlikely to cause annoyance to neighbours.

She was surprised to see as she passed that John hadn't put his forcing jars over his rhubarb and that he hadn't started his spring planting. He was usually the first to get everything underway and was almost religious about his rhubarb, so Josie worried that Mary's health had declined further, keeping John by her side. Josie needed to speak to him anyway about the upcoming AGM, so resolved to call to see him tomorrow, taking some daffodils for Mary.

Her own plot was also looking bare, but today she planned to plant out onions sets, garlic and early potatoes. Then, if she had time, she would plant out the early peas, broad beans, cabbage and lettuce seedlings she had started off in her greenhouse. Once they were in the ground, she'd have room to plant seeds of celery, French beans and cauliflower in her small greenhouse, all ready to plant out in the next month or so, once the weather was warm enough.

Over the next few days, if the weather held, she would also plant direct into the soil seeds of Swiss chard, early beetroot, carrots, parsnips and turnips. That sounded like a lot of work, but as the soil was already prepared, it wouldn't be too hard and she could leave constructing the wigwams of garden canes to support the growing peas and beans till a bit later.

She would also need to 'companion plant' flowers like calendula, cosmos, lavender, marigolds and nasturtiums before long to attract welcome insects and trap or scare off unwelcome ones. Well, that was her excuse for filling all the gaps in her allotments with flowers, but really, she just liked to see their cheerful colour in amongst the mainly green vegetables during the summer months.

The repetitive process of digging a hole and then planting a seedling into it freed Josie's mind to ponder the mystery of the ring. She was pretty sure it was an engagement ring, especially with that inscription, so she had started her search for its owner a couple of weeks ago by looking for an engagement announcement in local newspapers, using the British Newspaper Archive online at Kirkby library. Having found nothing, she then broadened her search to national newspapers, as a ring of that value was likely to have been intended for someone of wealth and status, so an announcement in the *Times* or some such was more than likely.

As she knew that the ring had been made in 1939, she had started her search that year, ending it in 1962 when Gerrard's father, who was believed to have done the engraving, had passed away. That search took her several days and frustratedly revealed nothing, but as the start of the search covered the war years, it perhaps wasn't surprising that people had other things on their minds and had not bothered with a newspaper announcement.

Her next tack had been to compile a list of well-to-do families who may have visited Kirkby Hall (and walked in the grounds and lost a ring). There were the obvious ones, the Howards, Duncombes, Nevilles and Lumleys, but it was difficult to find out who else may have been rich enough to afford such a ring.

As she planted, Josie's mind turned over the matter. She really needed to speak to someone with first-hand knowledge of the times, but it was unlikely that anyone from that period would still be around. Then it suddenly came to her, and she almost kicked herself for not thinking of it sooner as it was so obvious: Lady Kirkby! Dorothy Kirkby was in her late nineties, so definitely would have been around then, but also, she might remember visitors to the manor, especially one who had lost a fabulous ring.

Lady Kirkby was the Patron of the Kirkby Allotment Association because the land where the allotments were now had been her gift to the Council. She took a keen interest in the allotments, and in the past had always attended the AGM and had handed out the prizes at the annual produce show. Since she had become housebound, Josie called round to see her two or three times a year instead. Lady Kirkby liked to be given a formal report, but once that was done, they would then have a good old chat over tea and scones. Dorothy was always keen to hear about mutual acquaintances, especially births and deaths, new shops and any other changes to the town.

Having finished planting the onions, garlic and potatoes, Josies decided that was enough for today and that she would go and see Dorothy and plant the rest another day. She'd have to come back and see Dorothy after the AGM to give her formal report, but she didn't want to wait until then to see if she could get a bit further in solving the mystery. Knowing that Lady Kirkby enjoyed a good gossip and must be quite lonely, she didn't think she would mind her dropping in without an appointment. Josie washed her hands under the cold tap, tidied her hair, changed out of her wellingtons and walked higher up the hill to the manor.

It was an agency carer who answered the doorbell and she asked Josie to wait whilst she checked if Lady Kirkby was up to seeing visitors. Something about how she said it made Josie wonder if Dorothy was unwell, and she prayed she wasn't, not just because she really wanted to solve the mystery, but because she was very fond of the old lady. The carer returned almost immediately and told her that Lady Kirkby was asleep and she didn't want to disturb her unless it was urgent.

"No, please don't disturb her," said Josie. "It's not urgent and I'll come another time. Please just tell her that Josie sends her regards."

The carer nodded and closed the door leaving Josie to set off back home, disappointed not to have spoken to her.

The doorbell had woken Dorothy from a wonderful dream about her beloved Henry and she wanted so much to go back there that she had pretended to be asleep when the carers quietly peered round the door. Now the caller, whoever it was, had gone but she couldn't go back to sleep, so instead, she let her mind wander back in time and remember…

\*\*\*

The doorbell rang and she heard the maid answer it; she hardly had time to check her hair in the mirror over the fireplace before the morning room door opened and the Honourable Henry Neville was announced. Dorothy was delighted to see him, not having expected him today, and thought how handsome he looked in his uniform. He walked straight up to her and kissed her hands and she could see his face was pale and that he seemed agitated.

"Are you alright, my love?" she asked.

"Is your father in, Dottie, I need to speak to him urgently," he replied, not answering her question.

Dorothy shook her head, her heart racing not just at the sight of the man she loved, but at the urgency in his voice.

"No Henry, he and Mama have gone to London to visit George and will not be back until tomorrow," she replied.

Henry paced around the room for a moment and then seemed to come to a decision. He flung open the French windows and then reached out his hand to her.

"Walk with me, darling Dottie?" he asked.

She nodded and took his hand, and they walked in silence for a while, arm in arm, through the gardens, then wandered down the lavender bordered path towards the woods and the old carriage house. His hand kept returning to something in his pocket and she could see he was on edge, but still she said nothing, unsure of how to break the silence. Just as they reached the carriage house the heavens opened, massive raindrops threating to soak them, so they dashed inside the barn to shelter.

"Come, sit here a moment, Dottie," said Henry, talking her hand and leading her towards an old carriage that must have belonged to her grandparents.

He brushed the dust off the wide, soft leather seat with his handkerchief and then helped her in before sitting next to her and taking her hand.

"I wanted to ask your father something," he said, "and tomorrow will be too late."

"What did you want to ask him?" asked Dorothy, her heart racing.

"I wanted to ask for your hand in marriage," he said, looking deep into her eyes.

"On Henry!" she cried, throwing her arms around his neck.

She pressed her lips to his and it was several minutes until he broke away, leaving them both breathless and wanting more. He reached into his pocket and pulled out a small box before sinking to his knees in the small space between seats.

"Lady Dorothy Kirkby, will you do me the honour of being my wife?" he asked.

"Yes, oh yes!" she cried.

Henry opened the box and she gasped at the stunning ring as he gently placed it onto her finger.

Barely pausing to admire it, she pulled him onto the seat beside her and drew him into another kiss, even longer than the first, but then suddenly broke away, remembering his words.

"Why will tomorrow be too late, Henry?" she asked,

"My regiment is being sent to join the British Expeditionary Force in France tomorrow, Dottie. I couldn't bear to leave without knowing you are mine, knowing that if I don't come back, you would never know how much I love you."

"No, oh no! I can't lose you!" she cried, pulling him close and covering his face with kisses.

Tears were running down her face and he kissed them away. Their kisses became more urgent, and then, in the seclusion of the carriage, with the storm raging outside, they made love for the first, and last, time.

Much later, when the storm had ended and Henry could stay no longer, he showed her the tiny inscription inside the ring 'My one and only love'. She looked deep into his eyes and told him that he too was her one and only love and that there could never be another. He asked that she keep the ring a secret until he returned on leave and had the chance to formally ask her father for her hand. Dorothy agreed readily: as far as she was concerned, she was already his wife.

# CHAPTER TWENTY-ONE

The Allotment Association AGM was more a social event than anything else. Once the formal bit was out of the way, bottles of homemade wine would be opened to wash down the mountains of cake and everyone would have a good catch up and a moan about the weather.

Josie had been surprised that Councillor Smythe had deemed to attend, recognising his booming voice as he spoke loudly to an underdressed woman she didn't recognise. The councillor was probably in his seventies, mainly bald with just a few wisps of white hair and a beak of a nose. He was a head taller than most people in the room and never failed to use his height to his advantage, looking down his nose at people as he surveyed the room.

He hadn't had the courtesy to introduce himself to her, revelling as he was in the attentions of the woman who was hanging on his every word. They were standing so close that Josie wondered if she was his wife but couldn't make up her mind as, although of indeterminable age, the woman was clearly much younger than him.

Josie made a mental note to welcome the councillor to the AGM in her opening remarks, before taking her place at the centre of the table at the front of the hall. John was already seated, ready to give his treasurer's report and Kara, who would kindly take the minutes, gave her a thumbs up from her seat at the end of the table. Josie waited until everyone was settled in their seats and was just standing up ready to begin when Councillor Smythe walked to the front of the hall.

Turning his back on her whilst flapping his hand behind his back to indicate she should sit down again, he cleared his throat noisily.

"Ladies and gentlemen, it is my duty to welcome you to this year's Kirkby Allotment Association AGM," he pronounced. "I am Councillor Smythe, and I am the Chair of the Parks and Open Spaces Committee. As you will know, I am a former Lord Mayor."

He paused and looked around the room expectantly, until the blowsy woman he'd been talking to started to clap loudly. A few people half-heartedly joined in and he gave a self-satisfied nod of his head.

"This is Ms Greenwood, the current Chair of the Allotment Association who used to work at the local school," he continued, waving vaguely in her direction.

There was an audible gasp from the room. Almost without exception, everybody in the room knew and respected Josie, who had either taught them, or taught their children or grandchildren, and who at some point in the last twenty years had helped them become successful allotment owners. People began to mutter at the disrespect and Josie stood up quickly, not wanting things to get out of hand.

"Well, councillor, I was just a headmistress, and I'm sure your role as Lord Major was far more important, but with your permission, I'd like to echo your welcome and start the meeting."

Councillor Smythe was oblivious to her sarcasm, but there were a few smothered sniggers, especially when Smythe regally gave her permission to carry on.

The meeting then went on without a further hitch. Josie gave her Chair's report, briefly mentioning the cat scandal but not dwelling on it, making more of the success of the previous year's produce show and the support the Association gave to the local food bank. John gave a brief financial report and then left to get back to Mary.

Josie then asked allotment holders who were giving up their plots at the year end to let her know and, as John uncharacteristically hadn't mentioned it, reminded everyone that their annual fees were now due.

On behalf of John who had put it on the agenda, Josie then put forward a request to install CCTV. This was something that she was personally opposed to, believing that the allotments were somewhere where you went to get away from everything without worrying about who was watching you on a screen somewhere, but she still did her best to give unbiased facts to the meeting. Some concerns were raised about invasion of privacy, and, having had a similar discussion with governors and parents at the school when she was headmistress, she was able to explain that in in accordance with Data Protection legislation the recordings would not be viewed by anyone unless there was a good reason to do so and that they would be overwritten every 30 days.

A vote was taken, and it was agreed that, subject to finances, a limited system would be installed to just cover the entrances to the Allotments. It was also agreed that they would approach the Council for a grant to pay for it. Every year they had the option of a grant for infrastructure projects, but seldom took it, mainly because they could do most things themselves.

Josie looked around the room to catch Councillor Smythe's eye, as he may be able to confirm if CCTV was eligible for the grant, but she couldn't see him anywhere. She was a bit peeved that he had gate-crashed the start of the meeting but then hadn't stayed for a part where he might have been of some use.

That decided, there was no other business on the agenda, so Josie gave a warm vote of thanks to the local stables for continuing to supply horse manure free of charge, and to everyone who generously left surplus plants, seeds and produce on the 'swaps' table for anyone to use. There were then a few simple questions and answers, but very soon the formal part of the meeting was finished and the social part began.

"Who the hell does that councillor think he is? What a pompous ass!" whispered Kara crossly in Josie's ear as she handed her a much-needed glass of dandelion wine.

Before she could answer, the unknown woman sashayed up to them.

"Hello," said Josie, plastering on a smile. "I don't think we've met!"

At close quarters she looked older than Kara had first thought, with badly drawn-on eyebrows that gave her a look of permanent surprise. Her shoulder length hair was a strawy blonde and in need of a good cut and her too low neckline showed not just her ample cleavage but the frayed edges of a red bra. Josie though she looked like the archetypal barmaid but chided herself for being uncharitable: every woman had the right to dress how she choose without being judged.

"Hi, I'm Poppy, Poppy Gilbert," said the woman. "My parents must have known I'd be a great gardener when they named me after a flower," she simpered.

"Welcome Poppy. I'd like to think everyone has the ability to be a gardener, even if their parents didn't have the foresight to encourage them with such a lovely name," replied Josie with a smile.

"No, I am a *professional* gardener, not some amateur playing at it. I'm RHS qualified and have worked at Kew and at Harwood House," said Poppy haughtily.

"Well, that's wonderful Poppy, I'm very envious. What can I do for you?" said Josie, forcing her smile up a few watts.

"I want an allotment," replied Poppy.

"Well, if you fill in one of the forms over there," said Josie, indicating a basket of forms, "we will put you on the waiting list and let you know as soon as one becomes available."

"No, I have to have one now," Poppy demanded.

"I'm sorry Poppy, but I'm afraid there are a few people already on the list, so you will have to wait a little while."

"No, I can't wait," replied Poppy. "I'm in a flat without any garden at all and I can't stand it. I've got to have an allotment."

"Gosh, that must be hard for you, but I'm sorry, you'll still need to wait until it's your turn as there are others in the same position," said Josie firmly.

"Yes, but I'm sure none of them are in Witness Protection, forced to leave their own large house and grounds just because they did the right thing!" said Poppy in a loud stage whisper.

"Oh dear, you poor thing," said Josie. "I'll see what I can do."

"Councillor Smythe said I should have the plot where you had the stolen cats because I need a large shed," said Poppy, hands on hips.

"Did he now?" said Josie. "We already have someone interested in that plot, I'm afraid."

"I think my needs are greater," Poppy sulked. "I've had such a terrible time and this is my chance to turn things around!"

Poppy plucked a grubby tissue from her large handbag and wiped her eyes theatrically. Kara tried not to laugh at the performance, as she was certain that there hadn't been any tears.

"Look, I'll speak to him and see if he is happy to have another one. Can you fill in a form with all your details and I'll let you know?" said Josie.

Poppy walked off without giving her any thanks and Josie and Kara watched her go as she wobbled across the room on too high heels.

"Who the hell does she think she is?" hissed Kara.

"Well, it can't be much fun being cooped up in a small flat if you are used to something better, and I'm sure her skills as a qualified gardener will be a benefit to us all," replied Josie kindly, taking a much-needed slurp of her wine.

"Problem is, Jack had already asked me for that plot, but I had to wait till today to see how many plots we would have available," she continued, looking concerned. "However, I don't want to get the wrong side of the councillor, if, for whatever reason, he wants her to have that specific plot."

"Well, why don't we ask Jack and see if he minds, and if he does, tough for Ms Gilbert – he asked first!" said Kara.

"I'm sure he'll be fine about it," said Josie," especially as we have some plots with better soil just come free that I can offer him."

The social part of the meeting quickly got lively as more homemade wine was consumed. The dandelion was all gone but Josie knew better than to attempt the pea pod wine and went for the somewhat too sweet plum wine instead. Josie was pleased to see Ben and Zoe there and went up to say hello and thank Zoe for the 'Diary of an Allotment Keeper' blog she'd been posting on the Kirkby Facebook pages.

"I really loved the photos you took of Ben and Jack putting the shed up," said Josie.

"Yes, I think the boys have a few fans," said Zoe with a laugh. "I've done a simple website for Jack, and put a link to it on Facebook, and it's been getting lots of hits. I think he has picked up a few jobs as a result."

"That's great!" said Josie. "Pity he isn't here tonight as I wanted to publicly thank him for all his work keeping the common areas tidy."

"Well, he's got a big day tomorrow," said Kara, joining them, and bringing Josie a slab of lemon drizzle cake. "First day in his new job!"

"I'm so thrilled he got it, said Josie, "I think he'll be a great asset to the school."

"Yes, but it's a pity its only part time, but with the bits of gardening work he has coming in too, he hopes to be able to rent his own flat soon."

Josie grinned at Kara, thinking that Kara knew a lot about Jack and clearly had been spending time with him. Kara, knowing what her friend was thinking, diverted her by asking if she had said 'Hello' to Hugo.

"No, not yet," said Josie, looking around the room. "Where is he?"

"He was here a moment ago," replied Kara, also looking around. "We were just chatting about the pros and cons of mulching. Hmm, you must have missed him. Again!"

# CHAPTER TWENTY-TWO

It was a relief to find that there was no change in Mary's condition when John got back from the AGM. His sister, Alison, had been sitting with her, knitting and chatting away, even though she was getting no response. John thanked Alison warmly and saw her into a taxi, not wanting her to walk home in the dark.

Then it was just John and Mary again, the same as it had been for as long as he could remember but may not be for much longer. The thought made him feel physically ill and he pushed aside the ham and pickle sandwich Alison had thoughtfully left for him and picked up Mary's hand. He thought he felt her squeeze it back and his heart lifted.

"Funny thing happened today, Mary," he said, in as light a voice as he could muster. "I called into the allotment on my way to the meeting, just to have a look really. I expected it to be full of weeds, but it was neat as a pin. Not only that, but there were rows of seedlings planted and mounds that are probably hiding early potatoes. What do you think of that?"

Mary made no response, but John had the feeling she was listening intently.

"First, I had vegetables disappearing, now I have them magically appearing!"

He sat quiet a moment pondering.

"I think whoever took them is making amends. And he's doing a good job too. Not quite as straight as I'd have liked them, but it will do!"

John glanced at Mary and could have sworn there was just a ghost of a smile.

# CHAPTER TWENTY-THREE

Jack was loving his new job. He'd always liked children and had hoped to have some of his own one day, but sadly that was unlikely to happen now that he was getting divorced.

Over the last couple of weeks, he'd seen a bit of Kara's children and was enjoying being an honorary uncle. They'd gone to see the latest children's animation film at the lovely old family-run cinema in Malton and had a pizza afterwards. He'd gently teased the children about the ridiculousness of the plot, but then made them giggle when he'd acted out some of the scenes, complete with silly voices. Jack was upset that he couldn't pay for the outing, but Kara assured him he would pay for the next one when he got his first wage, which pleased Jack as it meant she was happy to repeat the experience.

He had been doing a few little gardening jobs, courtesy of Zoe's website and word of mouth, but the regular income of the teaching assistant job, even thought it was only part time, would give him more security. It was strange how, having been homeless for months and sleeping rough, you soon got used to home comforts again and he couldn't wait to get out of the B&B and into his own place.

In preparation for his interview, he'd had his hair cut neatly at the local barbers and thought it was money well spent as he felt lighter afterward, not because of the loss of hair, but because it removed the last symbol of being homeless.

He had worked hard to prepare for the interview, spending hours in the library using the community computer, reading the government guidance 'Keeping Children Safe in Education' several times and completing the Council's online Safeguarding course. He also took a book out which covered the difficulties children on the autism spectrum experienced in formal education, which was hard going, but fascinating.

He was prepared for everything, apart from the question that floored him: what had he been doing since he left his last job? There had been a long moment of silence whilst his brain scrambled for an answer which wouldn't lose him the job, but in the end, he just decided to be honest and tell them he'd had some mental health problems. The Headmaster and the Governor who were conducting the interview looked at each other, and Jack's heart sunk, but they moved onto the next question and then sat back and observed as a panel of eight-year-olds quizzed him about what he'd bring to their classroom.

Jacks 'Big Idea' was to get the children involved in growing their own vegetables and then learn to cook them, inventing their own healthy recipes to serve to their families at a 'show and tell' event. The children loved it, and so did the headmaster, especially when Jack explained about weaving nature and environmental projects in with the vegetable growing and sharing their produce with elderly residents and the Food Bank.

It had been an anxious wait to hear back from the school, but possibly thanks to Josie's glowing reference, he was offered the job. Due to his history of mental health issues, it would be on a six-month probationary period to start with, and he would be required to study for the Level 3 Diploma in Supporting Teaching and Learning; if, at the end of the probationary period he was found to be unsuitable, he would have to repay the cost of the training. Josie thought this was harsh, but Jack was exuberant: he had a job!

Jack would still need to do other work to make ends meet and had been disappointed not to get the allotment with the barn on it, as that would have been useful if he was to set up his own gardening business properly in order to subsidise his work at the school. However, he could see Josie was in an awkward position, so he had just told her it wasn't a problem and asked for the one next to it instead. She had been surprised, as there were ones with better soil further down the hill that had become available, but he liked being high up the hill looking down over the town and he wanted to bring order to the wilderness that the plot had been left in.

His life settled into a routine: mornings at the school and afternoons outside, either doing little gardening or handyman jobs for people, clearing his own plot or tidying up around the allotments. It wasn't just that he wanted to give back to the people and community who had helped him, but he found that creating order, doing something useful and watching the changes as plants grew and the seasons moved on to be calming and healing.

Jack was also finding the counselling sessions, arranged by the outreach project, to be very helpful. He began to realise that his mental breakdown, or whatever it was, although triggered by Julie's unfaithfulness, had been a long time coming. Under the gentle probing of the counsellor, Elaine, he began to look back on his life, recognising the life events that had chipped away at his mental wellbeing.

His parents had split up when he was just four and his father had remarried and moved away. Apart from the occasional, late, birthday card when he was small, he'd not heard from his dad again and barely remembered him. He was close to his mother, but he realised now that she was overprotective and he'd never been allowed to go anywhere on his own or sleep over at friends' houses. The only friend he remembered coming to his house had been Julie, who lived two doors down and he had known her since they were babies together at playgroup.

He hadn't really minded as he enjoyed being with his mum, especially being in their garden together where he'd helped her grow fruit and vegetables and learnt the best flowers to plant to attract bees and butterflies. His favourite early memory was sitting on a rug, birds singing against the background hum of bees, the sun glowing through multi-coloured flower petals and butterfly wings as they danced around him.

His mum had died of cancer when he was eleven. She must have known but had never told him, so her death had been a terrible shock. Thinking back, she'd been getting weaker and weaker for a long time, and he'd carry the watering can for her or bring her a mug of her favourite herbal tea whilst she rested in the shade under the apple tree. They'd buried her ashes under that same tree, and when he went to live with his grandmother he hated leaving her and their beautiful garden behind.

His grandmother, Rose, lived in the gate house of a large house that belonged to the National Trust. When the visitors had all gone home, Jack would roam around the grounds unhindered and pretend he was the Lord of the Manor. Grandma had been a bit of a hippie in her day and rules and bedtimes were all fairly relaxed, a contrast to the strict regime he had known with his mother. The downside of living in the grounds of a stately home was that there was no one to play with, so he'd cycle over to play in Julie's garden, from where he could see the apple tree in his old garden.

Just five years later, the combination of a drunk driver and an icy road resulted in his grandmother's death, leaving him all alone again. He couldn't stay in the gate house, but he'd had a little money left to him which he'd used to buy food and pay rent on a tiny flat in town, and although he was only 16, he seemed to slip under the social services radar. Julie was the only constant in his life, so it was not surprising when she moved in with him at 18 and they got married at just 21.

"So," Jack summed up to Elaine, "everyone in my life had left me, and when Julie, who had been the only constant in my life abandoned me too, that was the final straw?"

"Yes," said Elaine, "it's not surprising your brain shut down rather than process another loss. But you are stronger than you know, and you're back and building a new life for yourself."

Jack smiled thinking back on that session. It had been a breakthrough for him, and understanding what had happened, was helping him shake off the feeling of worthlessness that had always haunted him. The decree nisi had come through, so he was a step closer to being completely free of his old life. He was starting to become part of the local community and every time someone said hello to him in the street, he felt a little more accepted.

# CHAPTER TWENTY-FOUR

Zoe leaned back against the bench, closed her eyes and tilted her face to the sun. Being so fair skinned she had to slather herself in sun cream in the summer, but she could get away with this lovely spring sunshine, which felt so different to the fume-laden mugginess of a London spring. She was taking a break from planting seedlings out with Ben and had been photographing the apple blossom in the allotment's small orchard to post on her 'Diary of an Allotment Keeper' blog. The bench under the trees was just too inviting and she had sat and typed her blog as apple blossom drifted around her and the sound of birds and bees filled the air.

The repetitive squeak of a rusty wheelbarrow wheel disturbed her and she opened her eyes to see a blonde woman of indeterminate age making hard work of pushing a wheelbarrow laden with plants and seedlings along the grass path between the allotments. She recognised some of the seedling trays as being ones she had just left on the 'swaps' bench and was glad someone was making use of them already.

"Good morning," called out Zoe. "Lovely day!"

The woman stopped and dropped the wheelbarrow handles and then came over and sat next to Zoe.

"Hi, I'm Poppy," she said.

"Hello Poppy, I'm Zoe. I'm glad you are getting those seedlings into the ground," Zoe replied, nodding towards the wheelbarrow. "They'll need a good watering."

"I haven't much time just now," said Poppy "as I have to get to work, but I wanted to get them before someone else had them."

"What do you do?" asked Zoe.

"I'm a cordon bleu chef, working at the Sun at present," replied Poppy.

"Wow," said Zoe. "They have a great reputation – we've been trying to get a booking for months!"

"Well, they could be a lot better if they took on some of my ideas. I was at the Ritz in London, so I'm used to serving the very best to the very best people – not like here!" she sniffed.

"Oh, I don't know, everyone seems lovely here," replied Zoe, defending her new hometown.

"Yes, but well, I was brought up in Belgravia, so I'm used to slightly higher standards," Poppy replied in a patronising voice.

"A fellow Londoner then," replied Zoe, trying not to get riled by Poppy's tone.

"What I miss most is the men," continued Poppy. "There is no one under the age of 70 to screw around here!"

Zoe had just been taking a sip from her water bottle and nearly choked but didn't have time to compose herself and formulate a reply before Poppy nudged her and pointed towards Zoe's allotment.

"Now that's better. Wouldn't mind having a go on that!"

Zoe looked where Poppy was pointing, but all she could see was Ben who had stopped planting and was having a much needed stretch. As he did so, his lovely muscly stomach was momentarily exposed.

"It's true what they say about black men, you know," continued Poppy in a conversational tone, "so I suppose I could lower myself to have sex with him as there is nothing else on offer around here."

She sighed extravagantly, implying it would be a chore.

Zoe didn't know if she was more shocked at the racist comments, the predatory way they were delivered, or the fact it was her husband they were aimed at. She stood up and faced Poppy, hands on her hips, trying to keep her anger under control.

"I'll thank you to keep your hands off my husband," she said icily, before walking away, wanting to get as much distance as possible between her and this awful woman.

# CHAPTER TWENTY-FIVE

It was a beautiful spring day and Josie was pottering about in her small garden before walking to the church as it was her turn on the flower arranging rota. She wasn't particularly religious but loved the calm, cool interior of the Norman church, the sense of peace and continuity and the way sunlight through the stained glass threw a kaleidoscope of dancing colours across the stone-flagged nave, worn smooth by the feet of many generations.

She also enjoyed flower arranging, not fussy table flowers or wedding bouquets, but big, bold statement arrangements that over the years she had down to a fine art. The secret of large arrangements was the foliage; lots of interesting leaf shapes and different shades of green to give bulk, height and depth, against which just a very few bright flowers would be needed. Usually, Josie got her greenery from her garden, the allotment or from along the hedgerow, but at this time of year there wasn't much available. In her garden she had cut some glossy evergreen laurel and a few branches off her twisted willow that had some dangling catkins attached, and those would make a good backdrop for sunny yellow daffodils.

She still needed a bit more foliage and was considering walking through the woods to see what else she could find, when she saw the post-lady walking past and so popped back inside to check if she had any post. She had hoped for a letter from her daughter, but there was just one envelope which had the frank mark of the local Council rather than an Australian stamp.

Josie frowned as she opened it as it appeared to be an invoice from the Parks and Open Spaces Department, but that didn't make any sense as she paid her annual allotment fee by direct debit annually before the AGM and she knew it had gone out on time. She turned to the accompanying letter, which bore the signature of Councillor Smythe.

"Dear Allotment Holder, please find enclosed an invoice to cover the upkeep of the common areas of the Kirkby Allotments. This is in addition to the annual rent and will be levied monthly to pay the contractor appointed by the Council. You are required to set up a direct debit forthwith. Any arrears will result in your eviction from the allotment."

Josies mouth fell open in astonishment, but before she could begin to process the information, the phone rang. She picked it up in a daze but was relieved to hear it was John.

"Hello, John. How is…?" she started but didn't have time to finish before John butted in angrily.

"Well Josie, I'm astonished you would organise this without discussing it with me, and indeed, putting it to all the allotment holders first. You've waited until I've got more important things on my mind and then go behind my back! I *am* still the treasurer you know!"

"John, if you are talking about this letter from Councillor Smythe, I've just received one myself and it's the first I knew of it!" replied Josie, fighting to stay calm.

"What? The Council have just done this without discussing it?" he replied.

"It appears so," said Josie, drily, "and last time I looked, the 'common areas' were immaculate."

"Yes, I thought everything was looking spick and span when I was last there," replied John. "Sorry Josie, I should have known you wouldn't do something like this. I've a lot on my plate at present, and it was a shock, a final straw, but I should have asked you before blaming you. I do apologise," he continued, sounding almost tearful.

"That okay, John, I understand," she replied gently. "Jack took it on himself to look after everything for us and it's never looked better, so I've no idea who this 'Council appointed contractor' is, or why they think it's necessary."

"Could it be Jack himself? We know nothing about him, Josie. He has just turned up and wormed his way in, then he did work unasked and now he is charging us for it? Was it him that sorted out my allotment, because I certainly didn't ask him to and I'm not paying him!" said John, his voice rising and starting to sound hysterical.

"No John, I like to think I'm a good judge of character and I don't believe for a moment it's Jack. It was Jack's idea to tidy up your allotment, John, when I told him how poorly Mary was, but Kara and I worked with him on it."

"Well, I owe you all thanks. Very kind of you," said John, sounding tearful again.

"Our pleasure, John. Now go back to Mary and I'll try and get to the bottom of this and call you back."

As soon as Josie hung up, the phone rang again, and this time it was Kara, also wanting to know what the hell was going on.

"How dare that pompous oaf do this without discussing it first?" she ranted. "He was at the AGM and could have raised it then if the Council had concerns!"

"I know Kara; I just don't understand it. I know the Council can step in if we allow anything that brings the Council into disrepute, but a few weeds, if there were any, is hardly going to be headlines in the local paper!" replied Josie.

They agreed that Josie would ring the Council and try and get to the bottom of it, and in the meantime Kara would email all the allotment holders and tell them that this charge hadn't been discussed with the Association, and that Josie was looking into it and would get back to them as soon as possible.

After listening to a recorded message and picking the right extension, Josie was left on hold for ages being played annoying loud music on a loop. Eventually a female voice answered snootily.

"Councillor Smythe's office. Can I help you?"

"May I speak to the Councillor please?" Josie asked calmly.

"Do you have an appointment?" the woman asked.

"No, but I do need to speak to him urgently," Josie replied.

"I'm afraid you'll have to make an appointment first," said the woman and then hung up, leaving Josie flabbergasted.

Josie counted slowly to ten and then redialled. The same recorded message and inane music assaulted her ears as she waited, getting crosser by the minute. She could see the greenery she had cut for the church starting to wilt and wished wholeheartedly that she was in the still calm of the church worrying about nothing more than the perfect position for a twig to be placed.

"Councillor Smythe's office. Can I help you?" the same woman answered.

"Can I make an appointment to speak to the Councillor please?" said Josie as pleasantly as she could, not wanting to be cut off again.

"What is it connection with?" asked the women.

"It's about Kirkby allotments, and as I said previously, its urgent," replied Josie.

"If it's an allotment matter, then you need to speak to the Chair of the Allotment Association. All the details are on the Council website," replied the annoying women.

"I *am* the Chair of the Allotment Association," responded Josie in her poshest voice, fearing that she was about to be cut off again.

"Well, why didn't you say so! Putting you through now."

Josie was flabbergasted but had no time to draw breath before Smythe's booming voice came down the line.

"Councillor Smythe here. What do you want? I'm just about to go into a Council meeting so I can only spare you two minutes."

"Well Councillor Smythe, Josie Greenwood, Chair of the Kirkby Allotment Association here, and I sincerely hope this matter can be sorted out in a couple of minutes as there has obviously been a mistake."

"What matter are you referring to Ms Greenwood?" he asked.

"The matter of an invoice I have received this morning, Councillor," she replied.

"If you need more time to pay Ms Greenwood, you need to speak to the Accounts Department, Smythe said icily.

"I don't need more time to pay," spluttered Josie, "I need to know who authorised it and who selected the contractor!"

"I did Ms Greenwood, in my capacity as Chair of Parks and Open Spaces: now if you will excuse me, I have important matters to deal with," said Smythe.

"Councillor Smythe, as Chair of the Allotment Association, any matters relating to the Association need to be authorised by myself and I would only do that after discussion with my fellow allotment holders. You have no right to interfere in the running of the Association!" said Josie, starting to lose her temper.

"Ah, but I do, Ms Greenwood. This is council land, and if it's not being looked after, it is in my powers to rectify the deficit at the expense of the leaseholder," said Smythe smugly.

"What are you talking about, Councillor," demanded Josie. "Our allotments are very well looked after!"

"That not what I heard Ms Greenwood. Firstly, you allow criminal activities to take place, then you turn a blind eye to tramps sleeping there and then I get a report that you have let the common areas get into a disgraceful state."

"That is not true, Councillor. All the common areas are neat and tidy, weeds removed, grass cut and hedges trimmed," replied Josie.

"Ah, good. She's been busy then," said Smythe.

"She? Who, are you referring to, Councillor?"

"Why Miss Gilbert, of course. Marvellous woman. What that woman can turn her hand to is astonishing. Did you know she was a stunt woman in the Bond films? You are lucky to have her," said the Councillor before ending the call without saying goodbye.

Josie stood listening to the dial tone for a second, too stunned to move. The councillor was correct in that the council could make the allotment holders pay for any clean up if, for example, there had been a leak of diesel causing contaminated land, but she was pretty sure that didn't apply to a few weeds and there hadn't been any anyway. Who could have reported them to the council, and why? Probably the person who had most to gain: Poppy Gilbert.

Josie rung John back and explained the extraordinary conversation. He was quiet for a moment, thinking.

"Assuming for a moment that there was an issue and a complaint had been made, the council's first move should have been to speak to us about it and give us time to remedy the issue. If they were not satisfied with our action, they would then need to obtain three quotes for us to discuss. It doesn't look like any of that has taken place and therefore their charge is illegal," he said finally.

"I agree with you John. I'll write to Councillor Smythe and ask for details of the 'report' he referred to and copies of the quotes obtained," said Josie. "And in the meantime, I will advise allotment holders not to pay!"

# CHAPTER TWENTY-SIX

Jack had spent the morning at school helping the children write their names on the side of a toilet roll tube, tape up one end, fill it full of soil and then plant a single bean in it. All the filled tubes were then clustered together on trays and carefully watered. Some trays were put on a south facing windowsill and others on a table at the back of the classroom, so that the children could learn about how sunlight was needed for growth. Jack then taped a chart with all the children's names on it to the wall, ready to be ticked off as each seedling appeared.

With the afternoon free to spend on his allotment, his first task was to clear all the weeds and put them in the composting bays he had created from some old pallets he'd found dumped. Josie had given him instruction on how to make the best compost, but as that wouldn't be ready for a long time, he had dug in as much horse manure as he could get hold of.

Once the soil was weed free, Jack levelled and marked out a square area where the children could plant their bean tubes once the seedlings were big enough. The outer tubes would rot down and the plants would grow strong as their roots wouldn't have been disturbed. He'd have liked to set aside other areas for the children, but that would leave little room for him to grow the vegetables that he already had in the ground.

Jack decided to speak to Josie and see if there was another plot he could have for the children to use. Glancing across at Poppy's plot next to his, he wished he could have had that one as the larger plot would have given him more room. He could have used the barn to store equipment and maybe as a teaching space when it was too wet for the children outside. He had understood that Poppy was a professional gardener, but she only appeared to have cultivated a small area behind the barn with what looked suspiciously to Jack like cannabis plants. He could be wrong, and it was none of his business, but he was starting to get annoyed as the more normal weeds that covered the rest of her plot were encroaching into his carefully cleared soil.

She did seem to make use of the barn, and he regularly saw her trundling a large petrol mower from the barn down the path through the woods to a van, and then back again later. He assumed she must be doing paid gardening jobs which wasn't leaving her much time for her own allotment. His own gardening jobs seemed to be drying up, which was a disappointment, as his dream of his own place would remain on hold if he didn't have more regular additional income.

Once or twice recently, Poppy had used her mower to cut the grass on the communal paths: as he regularly cut them with the allotment's old rotary mower, he was surprised they needed cutting, and cross as her bigger mower was churning up the edges that he had carefully planted with bee friendly flowers. Not only that, but she dumped the cuttings at the edge of his plot where they were going slimy and smelly, as grass cuttings alone would not compost down well.

He saw Poppy going into the barn and decided he would go and introduce himself, just to see if the children could use a part of her plot that she wasn't using. He knocked on the barn door and heard her call in a somewhat sultry tone "Come in." Jack walked into the barn and was surprised to see that Poppy was only wearing shorts and a sleeveless top. Up close, he could see she was a lot older than he had first thought, with heavy makeup covering lines, that on someone else he would have called 'laughter lines', but on her looked more like frown lines. He wondered vaguely if she was menopausal as it certainly wasn't warm enough yet to be so scantily dressed.

"Oh, it's you!" she said.

She had clearly been expecting someone else, but still smiled lasciviously and moved closer to him. Jack felt instantly uncomfortable as she looked him up and down, her tongue flicking around her lips like a snake.

"What can I do for you?" she asked, placing a hand on his arm and wiggling her thin eyebrows suggestively.

Jack stepped back, feeling trapped, wishing that he hadn't closed the barn door behind himself. He quickly put his request to her about the use of an unused part of her allotment for the local school children to learn how to grow vegetables.

Poppy laughed. Not a pleasant laugh, but a cackle that brought an image of a witch into his mind.

"No way!" she replied. "I'm not having a load of snotty kids nosing their way around here. Now if there is nothing else…?"

Jack beat a hasty retreat, feeling like he needed a shower. He cursed himself that he hadn't mentioned the weeds or the grass cuttings, but he just wanted to get out. As he returned to his own allotment, he thought he saw a man in a suit come through the woods and enter the barn and he hoped whoever it was would be safe in there with her.

# CHAPTER TWENTY-SEVEN

Ronan and Lily were wide eyed with excitement at having a dinner party at their house. They had been helping their mummy lay the table nicely for five grownups and had laid two special places for themselves at the kitchen island. As long as they didn't touch it, they were allowed have their own pretty candle to make their dinner posh too.

The children knew Jack already as he often came around, though Ronan was a bit nervous at seeing Mr Brown now that he was his teacher! Kara had explained that he wasn't a teacher, but a teaching assistant, but Ronan couldn't see the difference. All he knew was that Jack made his classes fun and he wished he was there all day, not just mornings.

Ronan knew that the other two grownups were called Ben and Zoe and that mummy really liked them, but Ronan didn't think she could like them as much as she seemed to like Jack. Ronan really missed his daddy and wondered if he could ask Jack if he could be his second daddy.

The doorbell rang and both Ronan and Lily dashed to answer it. Lily got there first but had frozen, sucking her thumb and gazing at the couple on the doorstep. Ronan could understand why, as they looked like fairy tale characters, the lady pale and pretty with lots of bouncy red hair, the man tall and dark with his arm around the lady as if she was a precious princess.

Remembering his manners, Ronan said hello and introduced himself and Lily, before taking their coats and showing them into the kitchen.

"Hello!" said Kara, giving Ben and Zoe a kiss on the cheek and placing a glass of wine in their hands. "Welcome to my humble abode!"

"It's lovely," said Zoe, looking around the cheerful room.

Kara smiled, pleased at the complement. She knew it wasn't a patch on Ben and Zoe's lovely home, but since her husband had left, she'd taken time to make the previously muted masculine colour scheme more her. She had painted the kitchen cupboard doors in a soft blue/green and she'd found some pretty floral curtains that had the same colour in them but that also had lilac and purple. She had picked up the same colours in the fabrics she had used to reupholster the old dining chairs after painting them in cream chalk paint. There were a few of her own landscape watercolours framed on the walls and the fridge was adorned with the children's bright paintings.

The doorbell announced Jack's arrival, and suddenly the small kitchen seemed very crowded. Kara got everyone seated, apart from Ronan, who was going to be their waiter. Bowls of salad, plates of garlic bread and bottles of wine were already on the table and Ronan asked if they wanted "red or green pasta." Kara laughed at their confusion and explained that the adults were having pesto sauce, but the children were having tomato sauce, however, everyone could choose whichever they wanted.

Once the grownups were all served with green pasta and smelly parmesan cheese shavings, Ronan joined his sister to enjoy his own dinner, hoping she hadn't eaten all the garlic bread.

Jack didn't have a computer, so he didn't get email and being of 'no fixed abode', wasn't getting any post either, so didn't know about the Council's letter. He was shocked and upset when Kara told him about it over dinner, upset because he couldn't afford any extra payments, and shocked that the Council had said that the common areas were a mess when he had worked hard to keep them tidy.

"That's not all, Jack," said Kara. "Apparently Poppy Gilbert has been appointed as the contractor to look after the common areas."

"No wonder she hasn't got time to look after her own allotment," said Jack. "It's a mess and I'm constantly having to dig up the weeds growing into my plot from hers."

"You should have a word with her, Jack," said Kara. "The allotment rules require you to keep your own plot tidy and not cause a nuisance to others."

"I did go round to speak to her," said Jack shamefaced, "but, well, she terrified me and I beat a hasty retreat without saying a word!"

"Why, what did she do?" asked Kara, amused.

"She didn't really do anything, apart from stand too close, but I got the distinct impression that if I stayed much longer, she'd have torn my clothes off!"

Kara smiled, thinking that Jack made her feel like tearing his clothes off too, but somehow, she had the impression he wouldn't mind if she did. Her wandering thoughts were interrupted by an angry outburst from Zoe.

"That bloody woman! Oops, sorry Kara," she said glancing at the children who were listening open mouthed.

"Children," said Kara quickly, desperate to hear what was annoying Zoe. "You can get down now and go and watch some cartoons. I'll bring your pudding through shortly."

The children dashed off to enjoy this rare treat of telly and pudding even though it was already past their bedtime.

"Go on," said Kara to Zoe as soon as they had gone.

Zoe looked at Ben and then back at Kara and Jack.

"Well, I haven't told Ben this either, but I met her the other day and she was complaining that there wasn't anyone to have sex with around here. Then she saw Ben and said that she wouldn't mind 'having a go on that'."

Ben snorted with laughter. "Having a go on me? Like I was a fairground ride or a new bike!"

"I think 'bike' is how one might describe her!" said Kara dryly.

"Then she made a remark about black men having bigger 'you-know-whats'," continued Zoe.

"Well, that's true," said Ben with a grin, earning himself a slap on the arm from Zoe.

"Seriously Zoe, I wouldn't touch her with a barge pole," said Ben, giving a mock shiver. "I know what Jack means – she is scary. I didn't tell you this, but at the allotment AGM when I popped to the loo, if it's who I think it is, she was coming out of the ladies and sort of accidently/deliberately brushed past me, her hand managing to come into contact with my crotch."

"She's a menace," said Zoe, angrily, "a sex pest!"

"Do you think that is how she got the contract for the allotments?" asked Kara.

"What do you mean?" asked Jack.

"Well, at the AGM she was all over that odious Councillor Smythe and he told Josie she was a 'marvellous woman'. Do you think there is something going on between them?"

"Surely a councillor wouldn't be so stupid?" asked Ben.

"I would hope not," said Kara and they lapsed into silence thinking about it.

"Is he a very tall older man?" asked Jack suddenly.

"Yes, why?" asked Kara.

"Just I think I saw someone of that description going into the barn after I left," replied Jack.

They all looked at each other and burst out laughing.

"Yuck, they would both have to be desperate!" said Kara. "You've put me off my pudding now!"

"Pudding?" said Ben, his face lighting up.

Kara grinned at him as she got up to get the large chocolate cake she had made, and then fetched ice cream and a bowl of home-grown strawberries. Having served her guests, she took small pieces through to the children along with a dire warning not to spill any on the settee.

The conversation moved on, and it was much later, once the children had been put to bed and the adults were relaxing in the lounge with another bottle of wine, that they returned to the topic.

"The 'Black Widow' told me she was a cordon bleu chef at the Sun," said Zoe, and they all laughed at her nickname for Ms Gilbert.

"Well, that's strange," said Kara, "my cousin is head chef there and he's never mentioned they had taken on a cordon bleu chef. I'll ask him next time I see him."

"She's had a very hectic life to get qualified as a top chef as well as being a top gardener," remarked Ben.

"Smythe told Josie she had also been a stunt woman on

Bond films, which is even more extraordinary," reported Kara.

"That *is* extraordinary, seeing as she was out of breath just pushing a wheelbarrow!" said Zoe.

"I'm going to google her," said Ben, reaching into Zoe's bag for her iPad.

After several minutes he gave up after coming up with nothing on any of the James Bond websites.

"Pass it here," said Zoe, taking the iPad off her husband. "I want to show Jack the new Facebook page I've set up for him."

"Oh, thanks Zoe. I can only go online when I go into the library, and I've been too busy with the new job to pop in this week. I hope whatever you've had done attracts some more work as it seems to have dried up recently."

Zoe didn't reply, as she was frowning and flicking through pages. She silently handed the iPad to Ben, pointing to something on the screen.

"What the..." Ben exclaimed, before also flicking through pages.

"What?" asked Kara and Jack simultaneously.

"It seems you are being trolled, Jack," said Ben. "For every great review posted, someone called 'The Garden Venus' has put up a terrible one, some referring to you as 'The Tramp'."

"What?" cried Kara.

Jack had gone quiet, feeling close to tears. It was true he had been a tramp, but he was working so hard to make a new life and now it felt like it could come crashing down on him. He could feel the edge of blackness hovering around him, but then Kara took his hand and squeezed it, and the blackness receded.

"We'll get to the bottom of this, mate," said Ben, patting his shoulder, "and when we do, we'll give them a taste of their own medicine."

# CHAPTER TWENTY-EIGHT

The third quote for installing CCTV at the allotments had arrived, and Josie looked at it despondently; it was even more expensive than the previous two! She knew without asking John that they didn't have enough funds for it, but remembering how upset he'd been previously when he thought she'd left him out of the loop, she thought she'd still better run it past him.

However, knowing how poorly Mary was, she didn't want to disturb him, so uncharacteristically her hand was dithering over the phone when it rang, making her jump.

"Good morning, Josie, Lady Dorothy here. I wondered when it would be convenient for you to come for tea and give me an update on the allotments?"

Josie felt instantly guilty: with everything else that had been going on, she'd forgotten to call on Lady Kirkby after the AGM. They arranged for her to visit the next day which would give Josie time to pull together a written report. It was raining heavily anyway, so Josie resigned herself to a day of admin, but first though, she thought decisively, she would ring John.

Later, having written the report, Josie went online to search the council webpage for a grant application form, which had been John's idea to fund the CCTV installation. She was glad now that she had phoned him because he clearly needed someone to talk to. Mary's condition was worsening and the doctor wanted to move her into a hospice, but John didn't want to let her go. Josie listened patiently and let him come to his own conclusion that he must do what was best for Mary.

Josie sent the grant form and the report to the printer then searched for the photo of the ring Jack had sent her, enlarged it, and then printed that out too. Thinking about Jack, she decided to look at the Facebook page that Zoe had recently made him and linked to his website and to the Kirkby website. Josie smiled to see the picture of him and Ben putting up Ben's shed, both grinning for the camera and pretended to flex their muscles.

There was a newer picture of Jack on his allotment with a group of pupils from the school, all proudly holding up what looked like toilet roll tubes with green shoots sprouting out of them. Josie scrolled through the comments from parents, all saying how much their children had enjoyed the project and how great Jack was. Then there was a comment from someone called 'The Garden Venus', whose portrait was just a flower, which read "Would you let a tramp look after your child?"

Josie was furious, and not wanting to upset Jack, she rang Zoe to see if she could remove it before he saw it.

"Oh no! Not another one!" said Zoe.

"What do you mean?" asked Josie.

"Someone is trolling Jack," replied Zoe. "As fast as I take them down, another one appears. It started on his gardening website and has lost him work."

"Well, this could lose him his job!" replied Josie. "I know what parents can be like – if someone gets a bee in their bonnet about something and the school gate rumour-mill gets going, by the end of the week it will have grown out of all proportion. Jack's only on probation, and the headmaster could decide its safer to 'let him go'."

"That's awful!" exclaimed Zoe. "I'll set Ben on tracing the troll – he had ways and means through his work. In the meantime, I'll take Jack's website and Facebook page down."

The next day Josie put together a large bunch of daffodils and forsythia, added in some twigs with fresh green leaves just unfurling and tied it all up with a ribbon. Putting the bouquet and her report into her basket, she walked up the hill, past the allotments, to Kirkby Manor. She waved at Jack as she passed him, but he was intent on carefully watering seedlings so didn't see her.

Lady Kirkby was sitting gazing out of the elegant French windows when Josie arrived and barely noticed Josie being shown in by the carer. As always, Dorothy was beautifully dressed, her white hair in a neat chignon, and her face radiant and remarkably unlined for someone nearly a hundred. Josie thought, not for the first time, that she must have been a great beauty in her youth.

Josie gave her report, but Dorothy wasn't really listening, her gaze constantly returning to the view from the window.

"Who is that young man?" asked Lady Kirkby suddenly, cutting Josie off in mid-sentence.

Josie stood and looked out of the window. Jack's allotment was the one nearest to the manor, and Josie could see him clearly as he hoed weeds along the edge of his plot.

"Oh, that's Jack," she replied.

"What do you know about him?" Lady Kirkby demanded.

Josie's heart sunk, hoping that Dorothy hadn't heard any of the comments being made about Jack: cut off as she was, Lady Kirkby still seemed to know everything that went on in Kirkby and her opinion held a lot of sway. Josie filled her in on what she knew about Jack, emphasizing what a nice young man he was, how much he had done, unasked, for the allotments and how well he was fitting in at the school. Dorothy listened intently, not saying anything until she'd finished.

"He reminds me of someone," she said wistfully.

"Oh, and that reminds me," said Josie, reaching into her basket for the photo of the ring. "Jack found this, and I wondered if you knew who it belonged to?"

As she saw the photo, Dorothy gasped, all colour left her face and the photo fell from her fingers as she slumped forward in the chair, unconscious.

# CHAPTER TWENTY-NINE

Great as it was to have a roof over his head, Jack was finding living in one room difficult, so he was spending as much time as he could outdoors. The improving weather was a great help, and when he couldn't find anything more to do at the allotments, he walked for miles, exploring the area and enjoying the many signs of spring.

Bright, fresh leaves had appeared on most of the trees and the air was full of birdsong as they busied themselves nest building. The stars of wild garlic were already out in the woods, so thick it looked like snow, but with an overpowering smell that left no doubt about what it was. Jack gathered handfuls of fresh garlic leaves to give to Kara to make into pesto and put into salads and soups.

Sometimes Kara came with him, and he really enjoyed chatting to her comfortably about everything and nothing as they walked. He had this strong urge to take her hand and constantly had to stop himself, not wanting to spoil their friendship.

He'd been getting his benefits through for a few weeks now, so he'd been able to eat and get himself a few more clothes for work from the charity shop, including two packs of new underpants and more socks. This saved him washing out his underwear in the sink every night and hoping it'd be dry in the morning but washing his shirts and trousers had been more difficult as there wasn't a laundrette in Kirkby.

Kara has solved this by ignoring his protests and picking up his washing once a week to 'bung in with hers'. Jack found the thought of his clothes tangling with hers in the washing machine curiously arousing and did his best to push the thought away. His clothes came back clean and neatly pressed, and he knew he could never repay her kindness.

Having got his first wage slip, Jack hoped that he could treat her to a meal out, but then realised that his wage had been paid into his bank, and they wouldn't issue him with a new bank card or unlock his account until he took in proof of identity, including proof of address. The address of a B & B wouldn't do, but once again it was Kara who came up with a solution: just put down her address and she would pass any post onto him.

His wage wasn't much after tax, but to him it seemed like a fortune. Sadly, when he cautiously looked at small houses or flats to rent in and around Kirkby, he soon realised that without the additional gardening income, he may be able to just about afford the rent, but wouldn't have enough for the utility bills and still have something left over for food. He had his savings of course, but he didn't want to break into them as they represented the promise of buying a place of his own one day.

Jack did, however, splash out on a smartphone so he could return Kara's old phone to her, fully topped up with credit. He had swapped the sim card over to keep the same phone number, so that potential clients could reach him, and so that Ronan, when he was eventually given his own phone, wouldn't be bothered with calls meant for Jack.

It was strange re-joining the world of social media and Jack realised he hadn't missed it one bit. Zoe still hadn't reinstated his website or Facebook page, but he scrolled through the Kirkby website and responded to a couple of requests for handyman or gardening small jobs. A message soon came back on the handyman job, which was helping to clear out and board an old loft space. It would be hot, dirty and uncomfortable work and he'd much rather be outside, but it was work, and he arranged to do it the following week once the house owner had got the boards delivered.

He looked again at his phone a short while later and saw a response to his offer to help with gardening, but it wasn't from the homeowner, but was from 'The Garden Venus' saying that Jack had done a terrible job for her, and that they would be better using PG Limited Gardening Services who she had needed to bring in to sort out the mess he'd left behind.

Jack was upset, but reading it again, he knew the troll had made a big mistake, one that could hopefully catch them. A quick call to Ben and he thought the same: he already had a good idea who was behind it and this would clinch it.

When the phone rang a few moments later, Jack thought it was Ben ringing him back, but it was Gerrard at the Antiques Shop, informing him he had eventually tracked down the invoice for the engraving on the ring. He said that Jack had done him a favour, as he'd been meaning to sort the records out for a very long time.

"Can you tell me who it was, please?" asked Jack, eager to hear.

"The Honourable Henry Neville," replied Gerrard. "Just before the outbreak of the war it looks like."

Jack was silent for a moment, stunned at the name he'd just heard. "Any indication of who the ring was intended for?" Jack asked quietly.

"Unfortunately not, but as I registered the find with the police more than 28 days ago and no one has come forward to claim it, it is legally yours now," replied Gerrard.

"Isn't it classed as 'treasure' and belongs to the crown?" asked Jack who vaguely remembered reading something about that.

"No," said Gerrard with a small laugh, "it's not old enough. It's all yours!"

"Wow," replied Jack. "Would you hang onto it for now Gerrard, I want to keep trying to find its rightful owner?"

Gerrard laughed again.

"I thought you might, Jack. It will be my pleasure to have something my father worked on for a little while longer. Good luck!"

Jack decided to call Josie, who had promised to try and discover who the ring belonged to and see if she had got anywhere with her research.

"Sorry Jack, lots of dead ends," she replied, but she promised to look into the Honourable Henry Neville and see if that led her anywhere.

Josie was silent for a moment, thinking.

"I have a hunch Lady Dorothy Kirkby may know something about it," she said eventually.

"Would you introduce me to her?" asked Jack.

"I'd love to, Jack, but I'm afraid I can't. Dorothy is in hospital. They think it might have been a stroke, and at nearly a hundred, she may not recover," Josie said sadly.

Jack sat for a moment after they had said goodbye, looking out of the window at the street below. He felt unaccountably upset at the news of Lady Kirkby's illness and couldn't understand why when he'd never even met her.

# CHAPTER THIRTY

The noise and heat of the hospital was making it impossible to sleep and Dorothy was getting increasingly agitated. Every time she was nearly asleep, they'd wake her up to take blood pressure or give her medication. Her back and hips ached terribly with laying on the hard mattress, and she longed for peace and quiet and her own soft bed. She was annoyed with the patronising way people spoke to her, as if she was going gaga, and hated the tasteless mess of food they tried to spoon feed her.

"Come along, my love, just try a little more for me, and then we'll have a nice wash and make you feel better, shall we?" said the ward orderly.

"I'm not 'your love', I'm Lady Kirkby," she said haughtily, "and what will make me feel better is going home!"

"Not till the doctor says you can, my love," replied the orderly, handing her a plastic feeder cup of tepid dark brown tea.

"Do you have any Earl Grey tea and a bone china cup," Dorothy asked hopefully.

"Oh, you are a one, aren't you!" replied the woman, putting the cup down on the tray table just out of Dorothy's reach before pushing her trolley onto the next bed.

To shut out the light and noise Dorothy closed her eyes and let her mind drift. Later she wouldn't be able to say whether she was asleep and dreaming or just remembering, but suddenly she was back in the garden.

\*\*\*

It was summer and the sun was warm on her face, so she adjusted her hat, not wanting to encourage freckles.

She was doing her bit for the war effort, 'Digging for Victory', planting vegetables where only a short while ago there had been flowers. Both of the gardeners had been called up as 'able bodied' men, so the task of providing fresh vegetables for the house, and half the town, now fell to her and a couple of land-girls who came in daily.

Previously, the extent of her gardening had been deadheading roses and cutting flowers for the house, so she'd never really got her hands dirty in this way before. Dorothy was surprised how much she enjoyed it, watching the circle of life from planting a seed to harvesting and enjoying the fruits of her labour.

Since the terrible news that George, her brother, had been killed in an air raid on London, her Mama had thrown herself into her work for the WRVS. Driving an ambulance, providing meals for soldiers and the elderly or anything else that was needed and would keep her busy, gave her no time to grieve.

Papa was never home either: he'd been a Captain in the First World War and had lost a leg at Ypres, and he was now a Major in the Home Guard with operational responsibility for North Yorkshire. He spent a lot of time either in York or in London, usually staying at his club between meetings.

Her parents both failed to see that Dorothy was grieving for her brother too, and they also failed to see that, despite the rationing, she had been putting on weight. Maybe they didn't see beyond the loose smocks she wore for gardening and attributed her early nights with dinner on a tray in her room to tiredness from working hard outside all day. Dorothy hoped against hope that Henry would soon be home on leave so he could speak to her father. Although it would be a very rushed wedding, she wouldn't be the first wartime bride that needed a wedding ring on her finger in a hurry.

Thinking about Henry, Dorothy pulled a fine gold chain out from under her blouse and held tightly the ring she wore hidden next to her heart. She closed her eyes and relived the wonderful moment that Henry had proposed to her eight months ago.

A bicycle bell brought her back to reality with a jolt, and she shaded her eyes to see the post office boy cycling up the hill towards the house. Dorothy dashed to answer the door, hoping for a letter from Henry, but instead she was handed a telegram;

a telegram informing her that Henry would never be returning to her.

Much later that evening, when her mother returned home and couldn't find her, a search was made of the grounds. It was the cries of a new-born baby that led them to her, laying in a pool of blood on the floor of the carriage house.

The baby girl had been premature, and Dorothy's mother had the awful task of breaking it to her that the baby hadn't survived. Dorothy felt like the soul had been ripped from her body and howled, inconsolable, for days. When she was calmer, she asked to see the baby's body, but her mother just shook her head: there was a war on, there was no time for such niceties, the body had already been disposed of…

It was some weeks until Dorothy was well enough to go out into the garden to search for her ring. All she had left of Henry was the ring, but that too was gone, the chain broken at some point during that terrible day.

\*\*\*

Dorothy felt someone gently wipe the tears off her face and her eyes flew open to see Josie sitting next to her hospital bed.

"You were calling for Henry, Dorothy. Would that be the Honourable Henry Neville?" Josie asked gently, taking Dorothy's hand.

Dorothy just nodded, trying to adjust to being back in the twenty-first century, to being in a hospital bed and to her secret being out after all these years.

"Yes," she eventually croaked, and Josie helped her to a sip of water and waited for her to continue.

"We were to be married, but he was killed in the war," she said eventually. "The day I heard the terrible news I must have lost my ring. The ring you appear to have found."

"Well, it was Jack who found it, and he'll be delighted to return it I'm sure," replied Josie.

"Jack – the man at the allotment?" ask Dorothy.

"Yes, that's him," said Josie.

"Will you ask him to come and see me, please?" asked Dorothy.

"Yes, but first I need to get you home – the doctor says you're free to leave. Not a stroke, just a 'funny turn' brought on, I can see now, by the photo of your precious ring. Apparently, you're 'strong as an ox' and will see us all out!"

Dorothy smiled for the first time in ages, whether at the prospect of going home, the prospect of meeting Jack or of having her ring returned Josie couldn't say, but the smile was good to see.

# CHAPTER THIRTY-ONE

'Council of War Meeting, 7pm, Kara's' was the text message Jack and Josie received. When they arrived, the children had been consigned to watch TV, Ben and Zoe were already seated around the kitchen table and a bottle of wine was on the go.

"Right," said Ben, opening up his laptop. "Jack's troll. The 'Gardening Venus' Facebook page is just a dummy page – no posts, no profile. Jack isn't the only one who has been trolled by them, anyone offering gardening services within a 50 mile radius has been slimed in this way," said Ben.

"Glad to know it's not personal then," said Jack with an attempt at a smile.

"Oh, but it is Jack, it's very personal. Whoever it is goes to a lot of trouble to find out something about their victim. In your case, it was that you had been homeless. In someone else's case it was that they once had a drink problem – the fact they had been on the wagon for two years was, of course, omitted. Enough to drive the poor sod back to drink with the nasty things that were said," he continued grimly.

"That's terrible!" said Josie, shocked at what she was hearing.

"It is," said Zoe, angrily. "Trolling has driven some people to suicide. Facebook, Twitter and the rest don't do anywhere near enough to stamp it out!"

"Zoe gets very wound up about this," said Ben, patting Zoe's knee.

"Why do they do it?" asked Jack.

"Well, in your specific case, to put you, the competition, out of business," replied Ben.

"In a lot of cases, though, it's just bullying for the same reasons there has always been bullying, whether in the school playground, the office or online: to make some inadequate prick feel bigger!" said Kara.

"What can we do about it, in Jack's specific case?" ask Josie.

"Well, I've already asked for this person to be blocked and all such posts taken down," said Zoe. "Whether that happens, we'll just have to wait and see."

"Zoe's also posted comments exposing this bullying, but social media is of the moment, and sadly, it's unlikely that those who were put off previously will get back to Jack," said Ben.

"What about 'PG Limited Gardening Services'? asked Jack.

"Ah, that's where it gets interesting," said Ben. "There is one director of PG Limited Gardening Services listed on Companies House – a Miss Pauline Gilbert.

"Pauline?" asked Kara.

"Yes, Pauline," confirmed Ben. However, the address listed is the same as the address on the Council website for Poppy Gilbert's business address as the contractor appointed to the allotments.

"I knew that bitch would be mixed up in this!" exploded Kara. Without thinking, Jack took her hand to calm her down, and then forgot to release it, and they remained hand in hand for the rest of the evening.

"Could Pauline be her mother?" asked Josie.

"Possibly, but I had a walk past the address, and it's a very small flat above the chip shop so unlikely to be the family address," said Zoe.

"Do you think her real name is Pauline, but she just calls herself Poppy to sound more gardener-like?" asked Jack.

"Well, she did make a thing about her name when I met her," said Josie, "so I think that is a distinct possibility."

"That's not all," said Ben. "I searched for Poppy or Pauline Gilbert on Companies House, and Pauline has had a string of gardening business that have gone bankrupt – each under slightly different names. A web search found a lot of angry suppliers who had gone unpaid and very unhappy customers with half-finished gardens."

They sat in silence for a moment, absorbing the news.

"And this is the women we are paying to look after the allotments!" said Josie crossly. "Or not paying, as I haven't yet got the information that I requested from Councillor Smythe."

"Has she actually done any work?" asked Kara.

"She's taken her mower down the paths a couple of times recently," said Jack.

"The ones you had already cut?" asked Kara.

"Yes, and unfortunately she's cut down the lavender seedlings and other bee-friendly plants I'd put in along the edges of the paths," said Jack quietly.

"That's awful Jack," said Kara, squeezing his hand.

"Does PG Limited Gardening Services have a website?" asked Jack.

"Yeah," replied Zoe. "An off-the-peg piece of crap, with nowhere for customers to post testimonials, or believe me it would have been full of stinkers already."

"Do they have a Facebook or Instagram page?" Kara asked.

"No." Zoe shook her head.

"How do they get work then?" asked Jack.

"I think she badmouths all competitors on their social media and then direct messages the person asking for a quote and steals the business," Zoe replied.

"Sneaky!" said Kara.

"So, what are we going to do about her?" asked Ben, looking around the group.

"I know what I'd like to do to her," muttered Kara.

"I don't like bullies, liars and sneaks," said Josie, "but I couldn't condone revenge – sorry – it's just not in my nature."

"What do you suggest we do?" asked Ben.

"Well, apart from all you're already doing, getting malicious posts taken down and counteracting negative comments about Jack with positive ones, I think we go old school."

"What do you mean?" asked Zoe.

"Well, before the internet and social media we still got things done you know," said Josie with a laugh. "So, we use the community networks that are here already: the 'Friends' of the school, the WI, the local garden centre, Kirkby Environmental Group, 'Men in Sheds', the Allotment Association, the church flower ladies. We talk to them, put up posters and hand out flyers. We give talks at their meetings on gardening, being green, the health benefits of gardening etc."

Josie paused for a moment and looked around the astonished group.

"Ms Gilbert uses the internet only and hasn't any local connections," explained Josie. "We won't stoop to her level and insult the competition, but we will make Jack the automatic go-to person for gardening, endorsed by the established Kirkby community. What do you think?"

Josie sat back with a big grin on her face. Zoe stared at her a bit, perplexed at there being tools outside of her own knowledge and skills.

"You, Mrs Greenwood, are brilliant!" she said after a long moment, her face clearing into a matching grin.

"Right," said Kara, "who's doing what?"

The rest of the evening passed quickly as more wine was consumed and each of the friends volunteered for tasks. Zoe would design and print posters and flyers. Ben would speak to the Environmental Group and 'Men in Sheds', Kara would spread the work via the 'Friends' of the school and the garden centre, and Josie would speak to the WI and the church flower ladies. They would all speak to other members of the Allotment Association whenever they saw them at the allotments.

Jack would have to prepare talks on gardening and be ready to deliver them, a thought that terrified him! Despite that, Jack left Kara's on a high, partly due to the new closeness he and Kara seemed to be developing, but also buoyed up by the lengths his friends would go for him.

# CHAPTER THIRTY-TWO

At John's request, Josie filled the church with daffodils for Mary's funeral, every ledge and windowsill a blaze of sunny colour. On the font and altar, she created large arrangements of daffodils and pussy-willow against a background of fresh spring leaves and sprigs of rosemary, for remembrance.

The church was full for the service, Mary having lived in Kirkby all her life and known and loved by many. Looking round, Josie could see almost everyone who was a member of the Allotment Association, now or in the past, John having been the Treasurer for as long as she could remember. Until she had become too ill, Mary had always been at John's side at the allotment and at Association events, where she always went out of her way to make newcomers welcome.

There was a hush and everyone got to their feet as the coffin was carried down the aisle, John supporting one corner. He looked ten years older than when Josie had last seen him, and visibly thinner, his suit hanging off him. Once the coffin had been laid on the trestles in front of the altar, John stood with his hand on the coffin looking lost until his sister, Alison, took his arm and led him to his seat in the front pew. The organist played the opening bars to 'All things bright and beautiful' and the mourners joined in, singing the simple words they had sung since nursery school.

The wake was a simple affair, just tea, sandwiches and cake in the church hall. Josie recognised several of the cakes as Kara's and felt a rush of gratitude to her big-hearted friend. Seeing Kara across the room holding tightly to Jack's hand, Josie hoped fervently that her heart wouldn't be broken again and that she would have the happiness she deserved. Despite the nature of the occasion, Josie was pretty sure that Kara was actively engaged in 'Operation Old School', as she was introducing Jack to as many of the 'worthies' of the community that she could and a poster advertising his services had been pinned to the notice board.

Josie turned to look at John, who was sitting with a cold cup of tea and an uneaten slice of cake in front of him. He had delivered the eulogy in a halting voice, often choked with tears, and had spoken of Mary's love for nature and the pleasure she had got from not just growing their own vegetables, but from the allotment community. He had said how much she had missed being able to get onto their allotment once she became wheelchair bound. As Josie listened to him, wiping away her own tears, an idea started to form in her head about something they could do as a lasting tribute to Mary.

# CHAPTER THIRTY-THREE

It was a lovely sunny day, and after a difficult morning at the school, Jack was throwing himself into work at the allotment to get rid of his frustration. He had been assigned as the one-to-one support for Bobby, a little boy with Asperger's Syndrome, and usually they got on well, but this morning Bobby had had a massive meltdown and nothing Jack could do seemed to calm him down. All he could do was take him to his 'chill-out' space, a little den made out of soft fabric in a quiet corner, where Bobby felt safe and would eventually calm down and fall asleep.

As Jack worked, planting out his main crop peas, a last sowing of summer broad beans and an early sowing of climbing French beans, Jack ran through the events of the morning to identify what had triggered Bobby's behaviour. He knew Bobby needed routine, and this morning the class teacher had been off sick, replaced by a supply teacher, a man called Richard, whereas the usual teacher was a lady, Emily. Jack had to admit, that although Richard seemed nice enough, he did have a very loud, grating voice, whereas Emily had a gentle, musical voice. Bobby's hearing was very sensitive, and even a lorry rumbling past on the main road could upset him, so that might well have been a factor as well as the unexpected change of teacher.

Then there had also been the matter of Bobby being permitted to read his book on insects once he had finished his work. Bobby was extremely bright and he would usually finish his work well ahead of the other children: he hated doing nothing, so Emily allowed him to read his book once he had finished, as long as it was put away once the other children had caught up. Richard obviously hadn't been informed of this arrangement and had taken Bobby's book off him, shaking his head at Jack when he'd tried to intervene.

Without his book, Bobby started to pace round in circles, his coping mechanism when he had nothing to do: Richard telling him loudly to sit down was probably the final straw.

Jack resolved to speak to Richard about Bobby's needs before the start of class tomorrow and also to prepare a simple 'Bobby Manual' for any new teachers to be given in future.

Jack watered his tiny seedlings of sweet corn, courgettes and pumpkins and closed the cold frame lid to protect them, as the nights were still too cold to leave them exposed. That was it for today for his own allotment, as he wanted to check on John's which had remained abandoned since Mary's death.

There were a few aphids on the top of John's soft fruit bushes, so Jack sprayed them with soapy water, not wanting to use an insecticide. Other than that, nothing appeared to need doing and he suspected that Josie was popping round regularly too to keep an eye on things. Operation Old School appeared to be working, and he had a few jobs lined up over the next few days, but with nothing else needing doing today, he just had time for a little wander in the strip of woods that ran along the side of the allotments before he picked Ronan and Lily up from school for Kara.

Bluebells were just starting to appear in the woods: it would be a few weeks until there would be a carpet of purply-blue, but the odd early ones added pinpoints of colour to the green tapestry. Jack frowned to see grass cuttings dumped alongside the path that led to the road, smothering the fledging bluebells. If Poppy Gilbert didn't want to have her own compost heap, which in her business he would have thought was a great benefit, there was a communal one that the holders of the smaller allotments utilised rather than take up space on their own plots.

Jack spotted chewing gum wrappers dropped along the length of the path, and a then saw a used condom thrown down where the woods ran alongside the barn. He'd pick the gum wrappers up, but he wouldn't be touching that!

As he waited outside the school gate for Ronan and Lily a short while later, he wondered how Kara had managed to juggle childcare and working previously. With the occasional sudden emergency in her work at the RSPCA, it must always have been a struggle to make sure she was at the school gates on time, but somehow, she had always managed it.

Today she and Josie were at the Magistrates Court in York, giving evidence in the animal cruelty prosecution of Sean Watson and his wife. They had no idea how long that would take, especially if they got caught in the rush hour traffic coming out of York. When Kara had mentioned it, Jack had immediately offered to pick up the children, which had been a weight off her mind, especially as Josie, who was her usual 'go-to' babysitter, would be in court in York with her.

While he waited, Jack smiled and nodded to some of the mums he had got to know a little through working at the school. Usually they were very friendly, but today they seem to ignore him and he had the distinct feeling they were talking about him. He sighed, assuming that Poppy Gilbert had been at work online again but knew that Zoe would be on top of it.

It was a relief when Bobby's mum, Amanda, came to talk to him, her smiley open face turning to a frown when Jack filled her in on Bobby's difficult morning. They agreed that she would explain to Bobby that changes can happen, and help him work out coping strategies. She would also work with Jack on a 'Bobby Manual' to have on hand when changes happened at the school.

The school doors opened and the children streamed out, Ronan and Lily bouncing around with excitement at Jack picking them up. Bobby, as always, came out last and then ran towards his mum and Jack, throwing his arms around one of Amanda's legs and one of Jack's, unbalancing them so that they had to grab hold of each other to prevent falling over. Jack gently disentangled himself and said goodbye to Amanda and Bobby, before taking Lily and Ronan's hands and setting off for their house, swinging their hands as they walked happily home.

Knowing that it would be a difficult day for Kara, Jack planned to make the kids tea and then get a tasty casserole simmering in the oven ready for her whatever time she got back. They were still taking it very slow in their blossoming relationship, just handholding and the occasional kiss, but Jack didn't think it would be long before they took things further. However, with two children around, opportunities for privacy were few and far between.

Kara was obviously exhausted by the time she came home, so apart from asking her how it went and giving her a cuddle, Jack left soon afterwards to allow her time to unwind before she went to bed. Back in his small room, without the noise of the children or the open space of the allotments, he felt claustrophobic and lonely. The phone rang suddenly, and seeing it was Kara, he answered it happily: a cosy chat was just what he needed.

"Don't mess me around, Jack!" Kara said angrily, before he'd even said hello.

"What! I'd never do that, Kara," protested jack, shocked at the change from the loving goodbye only an hour earlier.

"Oh yeah? Then what's this all over the Kirkby Facebook page. You and Bobby's mum in an embrace!" she shouted.

"Me and Amanda? What are you talking about Kara?" said Jack in confusion.

"Just about every mum at the school has tagged me in on a photo, Jack, and a picture doesn't lie!" Kara exploded.

Jack's heart sunk. He had been betrayed by Julie, and he knew how much that hurt. Kara had been cheated on by her ex-husband and he would never put her through the same pain.

"Kara, is Bobby in the picture?" he asked desperately.

"What's that got to do with it?" she asked, still angry. "No. Wait, maybe. The picture has been cropped, but there is a blur at the bottom which could be Bobby's blond hair."

"Is the picture taken outside the school, Kara?" Jack asked.

"Yes," replied Kara, quieter now.

"Okay. Bobby had had a bad day, and I was talking to Amanda about it, when he ran out and grabbed us both round the knees, literally throwing us together. Ask the kids if you don't believe me – they thought it was hilarious!" he said, starting to feel angry himself now. "Let me guess who posted it: 'Gardening Venus'. Am I right?"

"Yes," she said, quietly.

"Know this Kara. I love you and would never, ever cheat on you. But if you don't trust me, there is no point us continuing this relationship," Jack said, choking on the last few words.

There was silence for a few seconds.

"You love me?" she whispered.

"Yes," was all he said, holding his breath, knowing that their relationship hung in the balance.

"Can you come back round Jack. Please?" she asked.

# CHAPTER THIRTY-FOUR

Josie had found yesterday's court case harrowing, seeing the photos of the poor cats and hearing the details of their suffering had upset her more than she expected. Still, justice had been done and Sean was going to prison, even if it was only for 20 weeks. Kara had explained that was a good outcome, as most prison sentences were suspended, and as Sean was also banned for keeping or breading cats for 15 years and had to pay a fine of £5,000 plus court costs, it was considered an excellent outcome. Sean's wife had been sentenced to 200 hours community service plus court costs, and also banned from keeping or breeding cats for 15 years, so Kara and her RSPCA colleagues were very pleased that they had taken the case to court.

Having had a restless night, Josie had spent an hour or more filling in the grant application form and was looking forward to getting out and up to her allotment, as she knew that the stress of the last couple of days would melt away as soon as she got her hands in the soil. She was increasingly thinking of giving up the Chair of the Allotment Association, just to enjoy having an allotment without having to do all the admin that went with the role of Chair. She had asked at the AGM for nominations for Chair, and as always, there had been a resounding silence before she was quickly proposed and seconded and everyone gratefully voted her back into post.

The biggest frustration this morning had been a phone call to Councillor Smythe's office to get a response to her request for details of how Poppy Gilbert had been appointed as a contractor to look after the allotment's common areas – something they didn't need or want. After the usual long wait being played annoying music, his rottweiler secretary had confirmed that Councillor Smythe was aware of the correspondence, but it was 'not his policy to respond' to persons who questioned his decisions." She refused to let her speak to Smythe who had 'more important matters' to attend to.

Josie was just addressing the envelope for the grant application when Jack called round. He had picked up the ring from Gerrard and was on his way to give the ring to Lady Kirkby. As well as wanting to show Josie what the ring looked like properly cleaned up, he wanted to ask her how he should address Lady Kirkby.

Josie laughed and then thought for a moment.

"Well, I just call her Dorothy, but then we have been friends for a long time," she said. "She is a bit of a stickler for etiquette, however, so probably best call her 'Lady Kirkby' to start with and then take the lead from her."

"Not 'Your Ladyship', then?" asked Jack looking worried.

"No, that's going a bit far even for Dorothy's sensibilities!" laughed Josie.

Jack and Josie walked up the hill together as far as the entrance to the allotments, stopping at the post office to post the application form on the way. As Jack continued on to the manor, Josie turned into her allotment, keen to get on with putting netting over her early strawberries to keep the birds and squirrels out.

Jack rang the bell for Lady Kirkby's apartment and waited nervously for the carer to answer the door. He was shown into a lovely room which had a high ceiling covered in intricate mouldings. Sunlight streamed through large French windows framed in heavy pale-yellow silk. Sitting in the sun's spotlight, gazing out over the allotments was a very elderly lady, silver white hair framing her face. She turned on hearing his approach, and the bright blue of her eyes stopped him in his tracks: his mother's eyes had been the exact same shade.

Lady Kirkby stared right back; colour drained from her face and her hand clutched at her chest.

"Are you alright, Lady Kirkby," Jack asked, his concern for her overcoming his nervousness and the strange feeling of déjà vu that hit him on seeing her.

"Dorothy, please," she said, taking a shuddering breath and motioning him to sit opposite her.

Jack sat nervously on the edge of the delicate antique chair, feeling disconcerted as Lady Kirkby (Dorothy, he reminded himself), continued to stare at him.

"Tell me about your family, Jack," she commanded after what seemed like an age.

Jack was a bit surprised, thinking she would have been eager to see the ring and then be rid of him, but he found himself opening up to her, feeling strangely at home and unselfconscious as he told her his sad life story.

She listened carefully, saying nothing, and when he finished she remained silent for a moment longer, appearing to be deep in thought.

"What was your grandmother's name, Jack?" she asked suddenly.

"Rose," he replied.

"And her surname?" Dorothy asked.

"Well, she was adopted, so she took on her adoptive parent's name, Neville," he replied.

"Are you sure?" Dorothy demanded, suddenly looking pale again.

"Yes, I'm sure. It's my name after all: Jack Henry Neville-Brown," he said.

Dorothy just stared at him, and then suddenly picked up and rang the bell on the table next to her.

"Could we have a glass of sherry, please?" she asked the carer.

"Are you celebrating something, Lady Kirkby?" asked the carer, raising her eyebrows.

"I think I might be!" she replied, suddenly looking ten years younger.

Whilst the sherry was being fetched, Jack took the ring out of his jacket pocket and silently handed it to Dorothy. With shaking hands, Dorothy took the ring from him and slide it onto her third finger left hand, where it fitted perfectly. Tears ran down her face unchecked as she stared at it.

"My one and only love," she said quietly, caressing the ring.

# CHAPTER THIRTY-FIVE

Having had to take down another malicious post the previous day, Zoe was furious to see Gardening Venus's latest post on Kirkby Facebook, titled 'The Aspie Mum and the Tramp.' Not only was it totally insensitive to Bobby, Amanda and Jack, but the insinuations would be very upsetting to Kara. She could see that several 'friends' of Kara's had made certain she'd seen it, and whilst Zoe didn't believe for a moment what was being implied, she knew that Kara's hard shell was only paper thin, and after her ex's infidelities she would find it hard to trust again.

Thankfully, a furious Amanda had soon posted back explaining the picture (not that she had to) and giving Gardening Venus a real roasting. Amanda also praised Jack for the way he helped Bobby, saying, that for the first time, Bobby looked forward to going to school. Several other mums who had been there at the time waded in, disgusted at the post, and then a few other parents posted praise for Jack, saying how much he was helping their children with their reading and confidence and what a lovely man he was.

One mum asked, "Who the hell is Gardening Venus, and what was she doing hanging around the school, taking photos when she doesn't have any children there?" Soon a mass of indignant parents were joining in, and Zoe grinning, thinking that the Black Widow had scored an own goal. Still, although Operation Old School was going remarkably well, Zoe decided that now was the time to work a bit of her internet magic and get their own back a little – Josie needn't know!

Firstly, she set up a dummy Facebook page under the name of Primrose, with a picture of a primrose as her profile picture. Next, she found internet pictures of unfinished garden projects, badly laid patios, half dead plants and weed filled lawns, and put them together in a montage, altering bits in Photoshop so that the colour tones matched and they looked like they were all taken in the same garden. Finding the post where

Gardening Venus had recommended PG Gardening services, she responded, attaching the doctored picture, saying this was the state that PG Gardening services had left her garden and warning people not to use them.

Zoe then set up another fake Facebook page under the name of Angela Armstrong, listing her hobbies as gardening and entertaining, using a profile picture of two full wine glasses on a garden table against a blurry flower filled background. She found pictures of lovely gardens and edited elements of them into a glorious tableau, and then Angela responded to Primroses' post, putting in a link to Jack's website, and saying she recommend Jack Brown as he had done a lovely job in her garden.

Zoe then went in as herself and 'liked' Angela's post, tagging in a few locals who she knew Jack had done work for and some of the school mums she had got to know through her friendship with Kara. Zoe then took a well-earned break and had her lunch outside in the spring sunshine. When she checked Facebook again, a couple of the people she had tagged had responded, saying what a great job Jack had done for them, with real pictures of his work.

Zoe hadn't finished yet though, as over her lunch she had come up with another idea. This time the indignant Primrose posted that she had been researching Poppy Gilbert of PG Gardening services and found that she had 'done the dirty' on homeowners before. Zoe put in snips taken from the Companies House website, arranged in chronological order covering the start-up and bankruptcy of the many variations of the company name. For good measure, Zoe added links to old online reports from suppliers and homeowners to whom Gilbert owed money.

By the end of the afternoon, someone had made the link between Poppy Gilbert and Gardening Venus and someone else had cottoned on that Gardening Venus's post had been done maliciously to discredit a business rival. The Black Widow was fast becoming the most hated person on Facebook and Zoe poured herself a glass of wine to celebrate a good day's work.

That evening, when a glowing Kara and very happy Jack walked hand in hand to the school to pick up the kids, all the waiting parents greeted them warmly. A couple of people asked Jack if he could come and give them a quote for some work and a bemused Jack arranged to do so. Having spent the day in bed, neither of them had seen Facebook all day, so it was later that evening, cuddled up on the settee, that Kara, casually flicking through Facebook on her tablet, saw the string of posts and burst out laughing

"Seems like Zoe has been busy," she said, passing the tablet to Jack.

# CHAPTER THIRTY-SIX

Whoever was at the door wasn't giving up, and with a sigh, John pulled himself out of his chair and shuffled to the door.

"Whatever it is, I don't want it!" he said from behind the door.

"It's you I want John, I need your help," Josie said loudly.

"Sorry Josie, you'll have to get someone else to help. I'm a bit busy at the moment," John replied, starting to shuffle away.

"John, I really do need your help. Only you will do. Can you just spare me five minutes? Please?" Josie said, not giving up.

She heard a long sigh and then the chain being taken off the door and the key being turned. The door opened a crack and Josie was shocked to see how bad John looked but managed to keep her face neutral. Although it was early afternoon, he was still in pyjamas and wearing a stained dressing grown that hung off him. Josie imagined it had fitted him once, but it now looked at least two sizes too big. His face was grey, he hadn't shaved for several days and his eyes where red ringed and heavy.

Before he could stop her, Josie stepped inside and past him, straight down the hall and into the kitchen. In contrast to John's dishevelled appearance, the kitchen was pristine, just how Mary always kept it, but unlike when Mary was alive, there was no sign or smell of any cooking. Without asking, she filled the kettle and lifted a Tupperware full of Kara's brownies from her bag and placed it onto the table, peeling back the lid so that the delicious smell escaped. Once she had made two mugs of tea, she placed one in front of John who was sitting looking dejectedly at the floor.

"Right John," she said, putting a brownie down next to his tea, "I have a problem."

John didn't look up, but he did pick up a crumb of brownie and put it into his mouth.

"Remember that ridiculous letter we all got about paying for someone to look after the common areas of the allotments?" Josie asked.

John didn't reply, but he did break off a corner of the brownie and pop it into his mouth.

"Well, I asked Councillor Smythe to explain how and why, and he didn't respond. I chased it up and got nowhere," Josie said.

John looked up and frowned, and encouraged, Josie continued.

"As you know, the only common areas are the paths really and Jack had been cutting those and keeping everything neat. However, Ms Gilbert, to make it look like she was doing something, has recut them unnecessarily a couple of times, and because her mower is wide, she churned up the edges."

"Ridiculous," John muttered, taking a sip if the tea.

"That made me think, if the paths aren't wide enough for a mower, they are not wide enough for a wheelchair," she said.

John looked up for the first time.

"I also thought, that if we paved them to make it easier for wheelchairs and wheelbarrows, they wouldn't need mowing, so there would be no justification for us to pay someone to do so."

"Clever," said John, picking the brownie up and taking a bite,

"So, this is where you come in, John," Josie continued. "We need to approach local building suppliers to donate the materials to make the allotments accessible. You were in the trade before you retired, John, so you have the contacts…"

"You want me to make some calls?" John asked, a spark back in his voice.

"Please John, if you would," replied Josie, not letting the hope in her voice show. "I had applied for a grant to put in CCTV, but it was turned down, and when I tried to reapply for money to pave the paths, that was also turned down."

"What! They can't do that!" exploded John, fully alert now.

"That's what I thought," said Josie, "Surely paths are infrastructure?"

"Of course they are, and I'd have thought that CCTV was too. Do you want me to have a word with Smythe?" asked John.

"Would you John? As treasurer you may have more chance of finding out why we are not eligible – Councillor Smythe refuses to answer my queries," said Josie.

"Who does he think he is?" demanded John.

"I really don't know, but I've had just about enough of him!" Josie replied.

"I'll give the Council a ring this afternoon," said John. "I'll just, er, have a quick tidy up first," he said, glancing down at his pyjamas.

"Good," said Josie, "because I've got a casserole in the oven, so once you've made the call, come round and help me eat it and tell me how you got on."

Josie left him to his ablutions and walked home, smiling. Alison had phoned her that morning and told her she was really worried about John, who wouldn't even let her in the house and was wasting away with grief. Josie had gone to see him with two goals: one, to get him eating again, and two, to get him interested in something. She seemed to have managed both aims and with any luck would have the added bonus of him sorting out funding.

Josie checked on the casserole and then phoned Alison to give her an update, but it wasn't much after that that John appeared, clean and neat and full of indignation. Josie barely had time to usher him into her little garden where a jug of homemade lemonade awaited them, before his outrage burst out.

"That bloody man!" John exclaimed. "Excuse my French, Josie, but I'm so cross!"

Josie knew he was referring to Smythe, as any interaction with him made her feel the same way.

"Start at the beginning, John, and tell me what you've found out," said Josie calmly.

"Well, after being on hold for ages I finally got through to his bloody secretary who wouldn't let me speak to him," he began.

"No change there," said Josie. "Not just me then."

"So, I rung up my old mate, Steven, in Finance, the man I send our annual accounts to," he continued. "Steven went into the account and said that this year's grant had already been spent!"

"What?" burst out Josie. "We haven't spent it!"

"No, but Smythe has. He had used the money to buy a mower and other gardening equipment for that bloody Poppy Gilbert!"

"What!" Josie exclaimed again. "We don't need or want her services, and even if we did, as an independent contractor she should be paying for her own equipment!"

"You're right," said John, "but that's not all. Also being taken from the grant fund is a monthly allowance for Ms Gilbert's fuel for the mower. So far she has claimed more than I've spent on petrol for my car in a year!"

"But she's only cut the paths twice! It would have been hardly any fuel at all!" said Josie, her voice rising with surprise.

"Could we be subsidising her other business activities," replied John.

"I don't know, but it certainly sounds like some kind of mistake or perhaps fraud. Surely there would have to be receipts, and someone would have to sign off each claim?"

"I asked that of Steven," said John. "Yes, and yes; there are receipts and Smythe has signed them off!"

"Can Smythe legally access and allocate our grant fund?" asked Josie.

"Good question," replied John. "It's never come up before. Do you think Lady Kirkby would know what the rules are, as she set up the grant scheme in the first place?"

"I don't know, but I know the man to ask her. Jack and Dorothy have been getting on famously. He calls round to check on her a couple of times a week, so I'll ask him to pick her brains next time he calls. She might be nearly a hundred, but she's as sharp as a razor so she'll hopefully remember the details."

Josie and John moved inside to Josie's cosy kitchen where she served the casserole. John ate hungrily and accepted a second helping, and whilst they ate, they discussed the idea of making the allotments more accessible.

"It's not just putting in wide paths, Josie, we need someone who is a wheelchair user, or someone with other disabilities, to be able to use the allotment once they get there. Mary missed getting her hands into the soil or being able to reach to pick a flower to smell," said John passionately. "We need the garden itself to be accessible."

He stopped for a moment, lost in memories, regrets perhaps that Mary hadn't been able to access the garden. Josie patted his hand and waited.

"It would also be lovely to have a sensory garden for people with visual difficulties – you know aromatic plants and ones with interesting textured leaves. At the hospice there was a blind lady and when Mary was asleep, I'd talk to her and she'd ask me to describe flowers. I used to take some in for her to feel and smell and you could see how that ignited memories and made her happy," he continued.

"Then there are children – future gardeners," said Josie. "Jack has been doing some wonderful work, but he's run out of space, and an area you take children into has to be safe, so away from tools and irritant plants."

"Garden therapy too," said John. "I read about it – people who are prescribed gardening for depression."

"Okay John, so we are not just talking about wider paths anymore, we are talking about a big project. Trouble is, as well as how on earth we could fund it without a grant, I don't know where we would put it – all the allotments are taken," said Josie.

"Well, there are and there are not," replied John. "I didn't mention it at the AGM as my mind was elsewhere, but at least five allotment holders haven't paid their annual fees, and last time I looked, there wasn't much happening on their allotments. I think we should ask them if they want to retain their plots or are happy to give them up for an important cause."

"Right, assuming we can find a plot or two to convert, how are we going to pay for 'Mary's Memorial Allotment'?" asked Josie, looking at John out of the corner of her eye.

"Mary's Memorial Allotment," John repeated, his face lighting up. "That sounds grand, Josie, a fitting tribute!"

"I think I can pull in some favours as you suggested Josie, and get the materials donated, especially when I tell them it's in Mary's memory, but the manpower and skills to do it are another matter," said John. "I do have an idea, but I'll need to speak to Hugo."

"The elusive Hugo!" Josie commented dryly.

"What! You haven't met him yet? Pity, he's a grand chap – you'd get on well," said John.

"How could he help?" asked Josie, curious to know more about the mystery man.

"Well, not so much him, but his son, David. He was in the Engineering Corp and he had both his legs blown off in Afghanistan, so he is now a wheelchair user," said John.

"How awful!" said Josie, "Poor man!"

"Yes, but according to Hugo, he hasn't let it stop him – hopes to be in the next Paralympics."

"Wow, but how can he help us?" asked Josie.

"He can't, but his army mates might be able to!" replied John.

# CHAPTER THIRTY-SEVEN

Jack was keeping Dorothy company, and whilst she had a nap in her chair, he was reading her local paper, circling possible accommodation. He was fed up with living in one room and longed for a kitchen of his own where he could cook the vegetables that were growing on his allotment.

More importantly, he needed somewhere where he could be alone with Kara. They never came back to his cramped B&B, especially as all of Kirkby would soon know via Joyce if they did. They snatched moments when they could, but with the children at her house he never stayed the night, apart from the weekends that the children were at their dad's.

The care agency had let Dorothy down again, so Jack had made her lunch and done a bit of cleaning and then they had played cards till she started to doze. Tomorrow afternoon he had a gardening job booked, so if the agency carer didn't turn up again, he would have to ask Josie to pop in and make her some lunch. Josie was very busy working with John on fundraising and planning Mary's Memorial Allotment, but he knew she would be here if he asked her, as she was very fond of Dorothy too.

Jack had asked Dorothy to explain the terms of the grant scheme, and, as Josie had expected, Dorothy remembered it clearly. She told him that she had invested a large sum of money nearly 70 years ago and the interest was available annually for the Allotment Association, and only the Allotment Association, to access funds for infrastructure projects. The council's only role was to administer the scheme and they had no right to access it directly. Dorothy had been incensed that her money was being misappropriated and had written to Smythe demanding an explanation and reimbursement of the funds: so far, she hadn't had a reply.

Jack heard the rattle of the post box and went to fetch the post for Dorothy: there was a couple of letters, one bearing the logo of the NHS and the other stamped 'JMA Genetics', and Jack worried that they might be some hospital test results and hoped she was okay. When he returned with the post she had woken and was looking at the newspaper adverts he had ringed. Her face brightened when she saw the envelopes, but she tucked them into her pocket and said nothing.

"Jack, I wonder if you would be so kind as to do me a favour?" she asked.

"Of course, Dorothy," he replied.

"You can see how unreliable the agency carers have been," she said, and he nodded. "I think I need someone to live in now that I'm getting older."

Jack smiled, as at nearly a hundred, she had been 'getting older' for quite some time.

"Do you want me to do an online search for companies who offer live in support?" he asked, pulling out his phone.

"No Jack. I want you to move in," she said, fixing him with a steady eye.

Jack stared at her open-mouthed. Dorothy told him that in the old days she had had a housekeeper who had lived there and cooked for her and her guests. The housekeeper had had her own apartment which had a little sitting room with views over the allotments, a tiny kitchenette and a big bedroom with an en suite bathroom.

The housekeeper had kept Dorothy's apartment clean and also looked after the communal areas of the other apartments. When she could no longer get a live-in housekeeper, a local cleaning company had taken over the cleaning side, popping in reliably each week and doing a good job, but Dorothy hadn't been as lucky with the care side. The only support available was from a faceless national agency and the carers changed from week to week and often didn't turn up.

"You know I never use the main kitchen, so you wouldn't have to use the tiny one in the housekeeper's suite, and I'm very happy for you to have your girlfriend to stay," Dorothy said, smiling at Jack's expression. "Don't worry, your room is at the opposite end to mine and I'm a bit deaf, so I won't hear a thing," she continued with a laugh.

Jack didn't know whether to laugh or cry. It would be wonderful to have space and comfort and somewhere to be alone with Kara. It would also mean a lot to him to be on hand to assist Dorothy, who he had come to care about a great deal. Two things worried him though: would she want him to provide personal care which he didn't feel comfortable with, and could he afford it?

"Don't worry Jack," said Dorothy, reading his mind, "I won't expect you to wash and dress me, I'm perfectly capable if I take my time and I'll still have a carer pop in every day. It would just be nice to have more of your good company, and to share a meal when you have time to cook."

"I'd love to Dorothy, but I'm not sure I could afford the rent: how much will it be?"

"Well, nothing of course!" said Dorothy, looking offended. "I don't expect my guests to pay!"

"I don't know what to say, Dorothy," said Jack. "That is so generous of you!"

"Just say yes, Jack," said Dorothy, covering his strong brown hand with her pale arthritic one. "It would mean a lot to me."

# SUMMER

# CHAPTER THIRTY-EIGHT

Ben and Zoe had just finished their 'Three Sister Planting', planting corn-on-the-cob, climbing beans and pumpkin plants in the same bed. It was something that Ben had seen on *Gardener's World*, and as they hadn't already grown any of the plants from seed, he'd had to buy established plants. Still, he didn't think that was cheating as it was their first year in the allotment, and next year, if it worked, they would grow their own seedlings to use.

Ben had explained to Zoe that Three Sister Planting was a companion planting technique, originating from the indigenous tribes of North America. The corn provides a structure for the beans to climb, eliminating the need for poles. The beans provide the nitrogen to the soil that the other plants use and the pumpkins spread along the ground, blocking the sunlight, helping prevent the establishment of weeds.

As they planted the corn in a grid, Ben (quoting Monty Don) explained to Zoe that it was wind pollinated so if planted in a row there was a risk that the pollen could just blow away missing the entire line. Zoe just grinned at him and didn't let on that she had googled it and already knew the right way it should be planted.

Once finished, and very proud of their efforts, Zoe and Ben sat in deckchairs in the sun, having a cold drink and sharing some of Kara's wonderful lemon drizzle cake that was being sold to raise funds for Mary's Memorial Allotment.

"Who's that?" asked Zoe, shading her eyes and squinting at a group of people coming through the woods towards Poppy Gilbert's allotment. Despite the heat, they were all wearing suits, apart from Ms Gilbert who was wearing even less than usual, with shorts that left nothing to the imagination, and an overflowing bikini top.

"The tall one looks like Smythe," said Ben, "I recognise his balding head and enormous nose."

Zoe nodded and they watched the group wend their way through the allotments. Poppy appeared to be acting as a tour guide, pointing out the view and the main road. The four men and one woman were all making notes as they went, turning to Councillor Smythe from time to time and nodding in approval at his responses. When they got closer to Ben and Zoe, they stopped talking and walked past without acknowledging them.

"Do you want my cake?" asked Zoe, holding the bag out towards Ben. "The sight of the Black Widow's wobbly flesh up close, and seeing all those suits slobbering over her has put me off my food!"

Ben laughed but didn't take it, knowing that if he ate her cake, his life wouldn't be worth living.

"I wonder what she's up to?" asked Zoe.

"Up to no good, I'm sure!" said Ben. "That reminds me, we never did get our CCTV installed."

"Yeah," said Zoe, "We generously set Ms Gilbert up in business with all her equipment instead, equipment I bet she is using for her other clients!"

"It would be good to prove that, wouldn't it?" said Ben.

"Yes," agreed Zoe. "Josie asked her about it, and Madam said she had two mowers, one she used exclusively for us, and one for other clients."

"Yeah, right!" said Ben, sarcastically. "Interesting that they are both identical!"

They sat and sipped their drinks and Zoe finished off the rest of her cake without realising it.

"I've been thinking, Zoe," said Ben. "I have a lot of surveillance equipment that I've updated so the old stuff's not being used now. A camera over the entrance would be very easy for me to install and it could link wirelessly to a laptop in Josie's shed if she ever needed to check the images. I could also fit a camera, for security reasons of course, to cover the less known access through the woods. That one may not be as obvious, but if we put up a sign at the main entrance warning of CCTV surveillance it would cover both."

Zoe nodded and squinted up the hill to the barn, where Poppy was just ushering her guests inside.

"Good plan, but we really need to be able to see inside the barn, to see if she has, in fact, got two mowers. Right now, I'd also like to be able to hear inside too…"

"Leave it with me," said Ben with a grin.

Having informed a grateful Josie that he would be donating a basic CCTV system to the Association, a couple of days later after he had seen Poppy drive off in her van, Ben set about installing it.

He fixed a camera in plain sight on a post so that it recorded the main entrance gate and then screwed a CCTV warning sign to the gate. That done, he took his ladder up to where the woodland path emerged next to the barn and affixed a camera to a tree in a less obvious position but so that it would cover the comings and goings via that route.

Ben walked around the barn to see if he could see inside, but all the low-level windows were boarded up. However, there was a row of high-level half-moon windows and Ben reckoned that if he put a camera high enough in a tree and got the angle right, he'd be able to see in. A directional microphone might also prove interesting.

# CHAPTER THIRTY-NINE

Josie was looking forward to meeting Hugo at last: everyone said that she would like him, but so far, their paths hadn't crossed. John had set up a meeting with Hugo and his son, David, to discuss getting sponsorship and a labour force to improve access and convert some allotments into Mary's Memorial Allotment. Knowing that David wouldn't be able to get his wheelchair down the allotment's paths, they were meeting at Josie's house where there was level access around the side of the house and into the garden.

John was there already, and on hearing a car stop, he and Josie went to the front gate to greet their guests. They watched in awe as David swung his wheelchair out of the car on a remote-controlled arm and then, by holding onto a rail in the adapted car, he propelled himself into his chair, using the strength of his arms only. He was a good-looking young man, with an open smile, blue eyes and thick brown wavy hair. Once seated in his chair, he propelled it forward with ease and then shook John and Josie's hands with a firm grip.

His girlfriend got out of the car and came and introduced herself as Yasmin. She was of Asian origin, stunningly beautiful with a waterfall of shiny black hair and a warm smile. David was clearly besotted with her, holding her hand once they were all settled in Josie's sunny garden. Josie poured them cold drinks which they sipped whilst enjoying watching Lucky chasing bees unsuccessfully amongst the flowers.

"My dad sends his apologies," said David. "He volunteers for 'Crisis Line', and they were short staffed, so he had to go in to provide cover."

Josie laughed, and explained to a puzzled David that she and his dad were 'ships that pass in the night.'

"That's a pity," replied David, "Dad would love you, and he could do with some female company to stop him becoming a grumpy old man!"

David went onto explain that his mother had left over five years ago out of the blue for a 'younger model', and his father, blaming himself that she hadn't been happy, had thrown himself into voluntary work to make amends, and had taken up gardening to give himself peace. John and Josie both nodded, as although their circumstances were different, they both knew exactly how it felt to be alone after spending years with someone you cared about.

Josie had been a little surprised that Yasmin hadn't helped David get out of the car, but later, when she was helping Josie fetch cake from the kitchen, Yasmin told her that she was a physiotherapist and had met David when he was recuperating from his injuries: her job had been to make him self-sufficient, and hard as it was for her, she had to continue to stand back and make him do things for himself. David was grateful for her approach, as so many people tried to 'help', which made him feel like an invalid, something he certainly wasn't.

Josie was very impressed with the young couple, even more so when David told her that his army unit had promised to come and lay paths and build raised beds for them, all completely free of charge.

"There is one condition, though," said David, and Josie's heart sunk, thinking that it had been too good to be true. "Keep that awful man-eater away from my mates!"

Josie laughed, knowing exactly who he meant.

"How do you know about her?" she asked.

"She nearly gave my dad a heart attack when she came up behind him and fondled his bottom when he was leaning over weeding," replied David.

"Terrifies me too," muttered John.

David had brought with him a list of companies that Hugo had contacted and who had promised to supply stone or wood. John had a similar list, and it was soon clear that, with the army's help, John's dream of making the allotments accessible in Mary's memory could become a reality sooner rather than later.

Three of the allotment holders he had contacted had agreed to give up their allotments for the project, and as two of the allotments were next to each other, that would work well. John's idea was to make those two into one large completely accessible allotment for wheelchair users to share and make the other into partly a sensory garden, and partly a safe garden for children to learn to love gardening.

With the materials and manpower now available, they would also be able to make all paths through the allotment paved to make everywhere more accessible, removing the need for Ms Gilbert's services, not that they needed them anyway. When they explained that to David, he was even happier to help if it meant he was helping keep his dad safe from sexual harassment.

# CHAPTER FORTY

Jack was so pleased with how well his allotment was doing. All the earlier preparation work had paid off and he had begun to harvest beetroot, broad beans, cabbage, cauliflower, early peas, lettuce, spring onions and spinach. He'd also lifted a few early potatoes and planned to serve them with some of his freshly picked vegetables at dinner tonight when Ben and Zoe were joining them.

It was wonderful to be able to return their hospitality at last, and even better to have a large kitchen to cook in. Kara would be in there right now creating a wonderful dessert, with the children 'helping' her and Dorothy looking on and enjoying the young company.

Jack just had time to sow some more beetroot and lettuce seeds to give him a continuous crop and then he quickly hoed between the rows of plants, checked for aphids and gave everything a good watering before tidying up and going back to help Kara prepare for tonight's guests.

As he walked up the hill, whistling, Jack thought about what needed doing next in the allotment: if the weather held, he would plant his seedlings of Brussels sprouts, courgettes, French beans, leeks, pumpkins and outdoor tomatoes into their final position this week. He reminded himself to ask Josie or John what the best way was to control carrot fly; he'd read about pathogenic nematodes, a biological control and wondered if they had tried them or they just resorted to covering the base of the plants. He smiled to himself, amused that he was musing on such things - subjects that would never have entered his head a year ago.

As he came in through the front door of the manor, Poppy Gilbert was just coming down the ornate staircase, looking like the cat who had got the cream. She stopped two stairs from the bottom and looked down at him.

"The servant's entrance is round the back," she said coldly.

Jack could never understand why people were nasty when it took the same amount of effort to be nice; rather than reply and tell her exactly what he thought of her, he ignored her and kept on walking.

"Oi!" I was speaking to you!" she shouted after him. "The manor is not for tramps!"

Jack's patience snapped, and uncharacteristically, he turned and snapped back.

"Is that so? Then what are you doing here?"

"How dare you!" she exploded, but Jack ignored her and kept on walking, letting himself into Dorothy's apartment with the key she had given him.

He closed the door and leaned against it, letting his heart rate settle and retuning himself into the happy atmosphere, the children's laughter echoing down the hall. By the time he entered the kitchen he was calm and able to laugh at the scene of devastation created by Ronan and Lily, and, by the look of her flour smeared face, Dorothy too. Kara was the only one who looked clean, calm and in control as she came over and hugged him hello.

"Don't worry, I'm taking them home shortly and Josie's coming to babysit," she muttered in his ear.

Well before Ben and Zoe arrived, order had been restored and the table set with Dorothy's best silver and glassware. Jack hadn't much experience with cooking for a diner party, but thankfully, the most expensive piece of meat he had ever bought was cooked to perfection, thanks to an excellent local butcher, Kara's skills and good luck. His home-grown vegetables were sweet and tender and a perfect accompaniment to the meal and Ben's bottle of wine was going down a treat.

"As good as you'd get at the Sun any day," said Zoe, helping herself to a second helping.

"Oh, that reminds me," said Kara. "I spoke to my cousin who is the chef at the Sun, and Poppy Gilbert did work there, not as a cordon bleu chef but as a simple prep chef. Even then, my cousin said, that was stretching her abilities and her wandering hands were causing an issue. However, before she was 'let go' for poor performance, she was caught with her hand in the till and sacked. Apparently, they suspected money had been going missing for a while, so they put a hidden camera in and caught her red handed."

"Wow," said Zoe, "she's even more despicable than we thought!"

"She was here, earlier," said Jack quietly. "Told me to use the servant's entrance..."

"The cheek of the woman," exploded Kara.

"Where did you see her?" asked Dorothy.

"She was just coming downstairs, looking very pleased with herself," Jack replied.

"Hmm. I've had some complaints about 'goings on' in the penthouse apartment whenever Mrs Morrison is away on business," said Dorothy. "I think Madam may be the reason."

Zoe raised an eyebrow and looked at her, but Dorothy said no more.

"If you were kind, you'd describe her as a 'Walter Mitty' character," said Ben.

Zoe looked at Ben and raised her eyebrows even further in surprise.

"But I'm not kind, and I'd call her a liar, a thief and a whore!"

"That's a bit strong isn't it?" asked Jack.

"Wait till you see the video," muttered Zoe, under her breath, but only Jack heard her, as everyone's attention was on Kara who was bringing in a magnificent pavlova, piled with fruit and cream. This was followed by hot chocolate fudge cake and a large dish of ice cream.

Just as he lifted the first delicious spoonful to his lips, the doorbell rang and with a sigh, Jack put down his spoon and went to answered it. Two policemen were standing there, and before Jack could ask if he could help them, one of them pushed him against the wall, twisted his arms painfully behind his back and snapped handcuffs on.

"Are you Jack Brown?" the second policeman asked, walking uninvited into the hall.

"Yes. What the hell is going on?" Jack asked angrily, trying, and failing to get free.

"That's what we are here to find out, sir," said the policeman. "We received information that you have taken advantage of an elderly lady of some means and are living in her apartment and holding her hostage."

"What!" exclaimed Jack, but before he could say anything else, Ben appeared to see what was going on.

"What the hell?" Ben exclaimed.

"Stay where you are," said the policeman, pulling out his handcuffs and advancing on Ben.

"Radio for backup," he instructed his colleague. "Looks like we've got more dodgy characters here!"

"You had better have a warrant and a very good reason to be here," said Ben in an accent that could cut glass. "Otherwise, I have a very good barrister who will have your bollocks on a plate."

The policeman stopped short, taken aback.

"Stand aside, sir. We need to see Lady Kirkby and verify she's safe and then we'll be taking this man down the station for questioning."

"I am perfectly safe," said Dorothy, appearing behind Ben on Kara's arm.

"Unhand my great-grandson immediately!" she demanded in a loud clear voice.

"Your great-grandson?" Jack and the policeman said simultaneously, staring at Lady Kirkby.

"Yes, my great-grandson," Dorothy replied haughtily. "Now, if you will excuse us, we are just about to have our dessert, and I'll thank you to leave immediately as I'm very much looking forward to it."

She turned and sailed back into the dining room, Kara mouthing "What the hell?" over her shoulder as they went.

Barely noticed the policemen apologising and leaving, Jack stood frozen, staring after Dorothy open-mouthed. Ben put an arm around Jack's shoulder and steered him back into the dining room, where Dorothy handed him a large glass of brandy, patted his shoulder and then tucked into her dessert without saying a word.

"That was delicious, Kara," she said, eventually putting down her spoon. "Is no one else eating?" she said, looking around the stunned group.

"Is it true?" Jack asked at last.

"Yes, darling Jack. It's true. I'm sorry you had to find out like this, but I'm glad you now know," she said, taking his hand.

"But how is that possible?" asked Jack. "I thought my name came from my grandma's adopted family, so how am I related to you?"

"That's what I have been trying to find out," said Dorothy. "I knew as soon as I saw you that somehow, miraculously, you and I were linked, but even though I've had that confirmed by a DNA test, I still can't work out how."

"I've had a DNA test?" asked Jack, confused.

"Oh yes," replied Dorothy dismissively. "If you remember, the first time we met you kindly shared a glass of sherry with me?"

"Yes, and…" replied Jack.

"Well, I kept the glass you'd used in a clean plastic bag, sent for a DNA kit, swabbed the glass and sent it off to a lab somewhere," she replied nonchalantly.

Jack just stared at her, and it was Ben who eventually broke the ice.

"Well, well, Lady Kirkby, you never cease to amaze!" he said.

Just then Kara's phone beeped to remind her it was time to leave to relieve Josie of her babysitting duties.

"Ring me," was all she said as she kissed Jack goodbye in the hallway.

Sensing that Jack was waiting for them to leave to talk to Dorothy, Ben and Zoe left almost immediately afterwards, thanking Jack and Dorothy for a wonderful meal and an interesting evening. Dorothy asked them not to mention her revelation to anyone, and they assured her they wouldn't.

"Well great-grandmother, we need to talk," said Jack, helping her up from her seat and leading her into the lounge.

# CHAPTER FORTY-ONE

It was Kara's weekend without the children and she and Jack had spent the morning in bed. They had barely spoken since Jack had arrived, having had more interesting things to do to occupy their morning, making up for it being two weeks since they were last alone together. Eventually another kind of hunger caught up with them and Jack went downstairs to make a tray of tea and toast. He'd added a pot of damson jam, bought from an honesty box stand outside a local house and a rose from the climber outside the back door.

"Breakfast is served, madam," he said, trying to bow without tipping the tray onto the bed.

"Just put it down there, Jeeves," Kara instructed.

Jack climbed back into bed and passed Kara her mug of tea.

"Actually, shouldn't it be me serving you now that you are the Lord of the Manor?" teased Kara.

"Ha, ha," said Jack sarcastically, swiping the piece of toast she had just spread with jam.

"So, tell me all about it," said Kara, settling herself comfortably against the pillows.

"Well, there is not that much to tell," said Jack. "The DNA test is 99.8% certain I am Dorothy's great-grandson, but that's all we are certain about. Poor Dorothy shared with me the sad story of her wartime sweetheart."

Jack was quiet for a moment, remembering Dorothy's great sadness and the tears she had shed that showed that even after all his time her grief was still raw.

"On the day he proposed to her and gave her that wonderful ring, they made love for the first, and only time, and then he went off to war the next day and never came back," said Jack.

"Poor Dorothy, she must have been heartbroken!" said Kara.

"She was, and she was also secretly pregnant with his child. The shock of receiving the news of his death put her into premature labour and she gave birth alone on the floor of the barn, or the 'carriage house' as she calls it. She nearly bled to death before she was found and taken to hospital."

"How awful!" exclaimed Kara. "What happened to the baby?"

"Well, that's the mystery," replied Jack. "Her mother told her the child hadn't survived, but she must have done, because otherwise I wouldn't be here."

"What a terrible thing to do!" exclaimed Kara. "Deprive a mother of her child, a mother who was already grieving for the loss of her fiancée!"

"Dorothy is finding it difficult to forgive her mother, but she must have thought it was for the best," continued Jack. "Dorothy was unmarried, and they were a family of some standing so I'm sure that her mother wouldn't have wanted shame bringing on them. There was also a war on, with all the risk and uncertainties of the time."

Kara nodded, understanding why, but like Dorothy, finding it difficult to understand a mother that didn't put her own daughter's happiness first.

"Her mother might have done it for the best intentions, in the hope Dorothy would meet and marry someone else in due course, which was more likely to happen with an unsullied reputation," she suggested after a moment's thought and Jack nodded in agreement.

"What Dorothy really can't understand is how my grandmother, Rose, ended up where she did, being brought up by her paternal grandparents," Jack continued.

"What?" cried Kara. "You've lost me now!"

"It's my name, Jack Henry Neville-Brown, that started Dorothy on that trail. Her fiancée was the Honourable Henry Neville, and she couldn't believe my name was a coincidence."

"Bloody hell, Jack. It's like a movie!" Kara exclaimed.

"It gets even more so," continued Jack. "Dorothy hired a private detective to find out what had happened, but whilst it's clear that Henry's parents brought up the child as their adopted daughter, there is no record of the adoption. She was in fact their granddaughter, but was never told that, always believing that she had no blood family of her own."

"That's so sad, and such a mystery," said Kara.

"Sooo," she said after a moment's thought, "your great-grandparents on your father's side, are actually your great-great-grandparents?

"Um, if you say so!" replied Jack, looking confused.

Kara sipped her tea and thought some more.

"Henry's parents had just lost their son. If I remember correctly, Dorothy's parents also lost their son in the war, so they must have known first-hand the pain of that loss. Do you think they gave Henry's parents his baby, a living part of Henry to ease their loss?"

"I don't know," said Jack, "but I like that theory, and so will Dorothy, as it paints her mother in a kinder light."

The couple finished their breakfast, put the tray on the floor and cuddled up, thinking about that time so long ago, and the invisible thread that had drawn Jack to his great grandmother.

"If I had your child, Jack," said Kara, seriously, "I would never let anyone take it from me."

"You'd have my child?" asked Jack, staring into her eyes.

"In a heartbeat," she replied.

They kissed passionately and then Jack drew back and looked deep into her eyes again.

"Kara, I know it's not possible just yet, but once my divorce comes through, if I had the nerve to ask you to marry me, can I hope you would say yes?" he asked nervously.

Kara's broke into a big grin and pulled him back up to her, covering his face with kisses.

"Yes, yes, yes," she replied.

# CHAPTER FORTY-TWO

With all the planning to make the allotments more accessible, Josie hadn't had much time for her own allotment and was missing the calming effect working the soil gave her. She had just one last task to do, and despite being desperate to get out into the sunshine, it was with some pleasure that she wrote to Councillor Smythe telling him that Ms Gilbert's non-existent services were not needed as there would shortly be no grass paths for her to maintain. Smythe hadn't had the courtesy to reply to her previous letter asking for details of how and why the contract had been awarded and to add insult to injury, she and her fellow allotments holders had received threatening final demand letters.

The Council's planning department had had more manners and had confirmed almost immediately that planning permission wasn't needed for Mary's Memorial Allotment and said it fitted well with the 'Town Plan'. Lady Kirkby had given her blessing, plans had been finalised, materials were being delivered next week and then David's army mates were coming the following week. There was a great buzz about the project and they had received lots of other offers of help, from allotment holders and the wider community, as well as disability organisations.

Jack had got the whole school involved in the design of the children's area, including a water feature shaped like an elephant which had water coming out of its trunk. The school's art and DT teacher was making it from a large plastic elephant bought on eBay which the children would cover in shiny mosaic tiles. This wasn't just a bit of fun for the kids, as the water feature would border the sensory garden and the sound of water, and the unusual shape to feel, would work well for visually impaired visitors too.

Also bordering the sensory garden, in a quiet corner under a tree, Jack had come up with the idea for a cocoon shaped chair hanging from the tree and surrounded by long rustling grasses as a meditative spot for visitors, but also as a chill out safe space for Bobby. His mother, Amanda, had loved the idea and managed to get the chair donated by a large garden centre in York. The grasses were being donated by Kirkby's own garden centre and a large local lavender farm were kindly giving lots of plants which would be used to line the paths so that their perfume would guide you around the garden.

To support Bobby's insect obsession, Jack had helped Bobby design 'insect hotels', before simplifying the design so that each child could make one of their own to place around the garden. The children were also making birdfeeders from recycled materials and Jack had made a couple of hedgehog boxes. The children had been doing paintings of everything they hoped to see in the garden and the best pictures would be used as part of an information leaflet about the garden which would go on the allotment's notice board.

As she walked up the hill, Josie smiled thinking about the project, and the difference it would make to a lot of people, herself included. She knew she had been getting a bit set in her ways, and if she was honest, a bit lonely, despite Lucky's company. Having a project to manage and new people to meet was just the tonic she needed, but in the meantime, there was a lot to do on her own allotment as everything had accelerated due to the good weather.

Josie began with harvesting some beetroot, broad beans, cabbage, lettuce and early potatoes and then picked the very first of her tomatoes, before filling a big Tupperware with juicy, ripe strawberries.

Even though it seemed a strange thing to be doing on a hot summer's day, Josie's next task was planting the seeds of her overwinter crops of kales, spring cabbage and spinach. Her other overwinter crops seedlings were more than ready to be planted out, so that was her next task before covering them with netting to help protect them from the birds.

Josie liked the way you had to plan and plant ahead, and she would always be thinking about the next season whilst enjoying the current one. It was one of the joys of gardening for her, the certainty that no matter what, the spring would follow the winter and the summer would follow the spring. Sometimes the spring was very late, sometimes the summers cool and the winters mild, but the seasons always rotated and you always needed to be ready for them. Josie found the circle of the gardening year comforting: next year at more or less the same time, she would be planting and harvesting the same crops, hopefully having learnt from any mistakes made this year. She knew eventually she would get too old, but the seasons would still be cycling and another gardener would be standing where she was now, continuing to work the soil.

Josie straightened up at last, arching her back to stretch out the ache and looked around. She could see John working on his allotment, and smiled, glad to see him back there again. If she wasn't mistaken, he was putting a piece of glass supported on bricks under each of his marrows to stop the underside going yellow or rotting. He was obviously hoping to get some good ones for the annual produce show in the autumn, to keep the 'biggest marrow' trophy he had won for the last five years.

She'd almost forgotten about the produce show this year with everything else going on and realised that was another marker in the passing of the year. Looking around her garden, Josie didn't think that she'd have anything worth entering, but regardless, would still enter most classes because it made people happy to beat the Association's Chair. Josie thought she would sponsor a new class at the show this year for all local children to enter, even those whose parents didn't have an allotment.

As she walked home with her heavy basket of produce, she passed some men in hi-vis jackets, one standing at the bottom corner of the allotments peering through a theodolite, focusing it on the staff being held by his colleague near the allotment entrance. She wondered if some roadworks were planned and glanced at the logos on their jackets as she passed; they were from some company she didn't know, not the highway agency, so hopefully that meant that no roadworks would hold up the work on Mary's Memorial Allotment.

# CHAPTER FORTY-THREE

Josie had expected half a dozen of David's army mates to come and help, so she was astonished when three large army trucks rolled up and a whole platoon jumped out and lined up on the pavement. David grinned when he saw them and saluted the lieutenant in command, before introducing him to Josie and John. Whilst he went over the plans with them, the men began unloading equipment and in a very short time the work was underway.

Jack had already dug up what was left of the lavender and other bee attracting plants he had planted along the paths so that they could be replanted in the sensory garden. The soldiers started by marking out the wider paths, removing the turf and then levelling the ground, before spreading a sub-base and tamping it down. Whilst this was going on, a small group began the work of making two allotments into one for the accessible garden and removing anything that wasn't needed from there and from what would be the children's / sensory garden.

Working alongside the army was a large group of local volunteers, preserving plants that could be reused, taking rubbish to the two large skips parked on the roadside and providing cold drinks and cake to the workers. Jack had the day off work, and he and Ben, as they were now experts, were erecting the accessible shed. Ben was stripped to the waist and Zoe was amused at the number of female volunteers who kindly brought him cold drinks as he sweated in the sunshine. She was less amused when she saw Poppy approaching, not wearing much more than Ben, with her tongue almost hanging out as she surveyed the sea of fit young men.

Josie had seen her too, and mindful of her promise to David went to intercept her.

"Good morning Poppy; have you come to help?" she asked, standing squarely in front of Poppy.

"Nah: too hot for work. I've just come to enjoy the view!" replied Poppy, trying to push past Josie.

"I'm afraid I'm going to have to ask you to leave, or at least remain on your own allotment only," replied Josie, standing her ground.

"Who the hell do you think you are, telling me what to do?" said Poppy, glaring at Josie.

"I'm the Chair of the Allotment Association and as such I am responsible for the safety of the allotments holders and all our kind volunteers today," replied Josie. "For their wellbeing, I'm asking you to leave."

"What the fuck do you mean?" spat Poppy.

"I've had complaints about you sexually harassing men, Ms Gilbert, and I can't allow that behaviour. Harassment of men or women is not acceptable anywhere, but especially not here where the allotments are a sanctuary for many people," Josie replied calmly.

"Harassment! What are you talking about, you dried-up old hag? They love it – can't get enough of me!" Poppy replied angrily, hitting out and catching Josie hard on the shoulder. Josie stumbled off the path, twisting her ankle and would have fallen if Jack hadn't caught her. Ben, who had also come to help when he and Jack saw the confrontation, stepped in front of Josie, blocking Poppy's path. He held up his phone, on which he'd been videoing the altercation.

"That's assault, Gilbert. Piss off to whatever sewer you crawled out off before I call the police!"

Poppy stood her ground a moment, raking Ben's glistening body with her eyes, before turning without a word and flouncing back to her allotment.

"Yuck! I think I need a shower," said Ben, shuddering theatrically.

"Are you okay Josie?" he asked, seeing her pale face. "You were magnificent!"

"I'm fine, Ben, and you were pretty impressive yourself!" she replied, taking a deep breath to calm herself.

"What you need is some of Kara's cake," said Jack, taking Josie's arm and helping her as she limped towards a bench in the shade.

Josie sat for a while and watched the work progressing, astounded at the speed the paths were being laid, with flags being passed from hand to hand in a highly efficient chain. Her shoulder and ankle were throbbing, and she felt a bit shaky as she didn't like confrontation; even when she was a headmistress, she had always managed to defuse situations with calmness and politeness. She was surprised how much Poppy's words had upset her and she tried to rationalise why. It wasn't being called an 'old hag' that bothered her but being called a 'dried up' old hag, a 'has been', past being loved or lovable.

She and Keith had had a warm and loving relationship but there hadn't been anyone since his death, so maybe Poppy was right? Josie had always thought that there could never be anyone else for her but wondered now if that was true. Could she love again? A strange feeling of hope flared in her heart, and she laughed out loud when the lieutenant told one of his men to ask this 'lovely young lady' to move so that they could lay flags alongside where she was sitting.

By the end of the day, all the paths were laid, the shed built, water feature installed, raised beds constructed and the basic layout of the two gardens in place. Tomorrow, soil would be delivered for the raised beds, and allotment volunteers would paint the shed 'Allotment Green' and plant up the sensory garden and children's area.

On the request of the lieutenant, David was the first wheelchair user to access the site, the soldiers forming an honour guard along the paths they had just laid. Josie glanced at Yasmin, who had tears in her eyes as she watched David reach his dad's allotment for the first time. Josie wished that Hugo could have been there to welcome him, but unfortunately, he was on shift at Crisis Line again. She hoped he would be at the allotments the following day to help, so she could meet him at last and tell him what a fine young man his son was.

Sadly, the next day, Josie couldn't put weight on her foot and spent the day reading with her leg raised, a bag of frozen peas wrapped in a tea towel draped over her ankle. Her shoulder was also sore, so having hopped into the kitchen to make a cup of tea, she had difficulty lifting the kettle and splashed cold water all over herself. Josie struggled upstairs to change, her eyes filling with tears, wishing that, for once, she had someone to look after her. She gave herself a talking to, but decided that as she was being so pathetic, she might as well just go to bed.

# CHAPTER FORTY-FOUR

The last week of term before the summer holidays arrived at last and the older children were setting off on their much-anticipated trip to Disneyland Paris. Ronan was in the class that was going, and as Jack had been asked to go to give one-to-one support for Bobby, Kara and a sulking Lily were left behind as the coach carrying their 'boys' pulled out of the school car park.

"It's not fair!" said Lily, stamping her feet.

"Life's not fair, Lily, but you'll get your turn in a couple of years' time," replied Kara soothingly.

"Anyway, we are going to have some girl time, Lily, so put that lip away and let's go and get some pampering!"

Lily cheered up immediately, being a very girly girl, and they made their way to the hairdressers to see if they could fit them in for their nails doing. Someone was in front of them at the reception desk, and as they waited their turn, Kara couldn't help overhearing as the angry customer raised her voice.

"What do you mean, you can't do a vajazzle?" said the woman, and Kara instantly recognised the voice as Poppy's. "I have an important meeting this afternoon and I need to look my best!"

"I'm sorry madam," replied the beautician. "We are a small-town hairdresser and there has been no call for, um, more personal adornment before. You would need to go into York, I think. Now if there wasn't anything else?"

"I haven't time to go to York," Poppy exploded.

"Excuse me," said Kara, tapping her on the shoulder. "The newsagent's sell glitter and glue, if that's any help? Better make sure it's the non-toxic glue – don't want to poison your colleague."

"Glitter!" said Lily, not giving a furious Poppy time to answer. "Can I do a vajazzle too, Mummy?"

As Poppy banged out of the shop, Kara and the beautician broke into hysterical laughter, made worse by Lily jumping up and down shouting 'vajazzle' over and over again. Once they had calmed down and Lily had chosen a shocking pink nail varnish, the beautician kept bursting into laughter again and there was soon more nail varnish around Lily's fingers than on her nails. Lily didn't mind, and as the beautician refused to let Kara pay, she took Lily to the café for a large knickerbocker glory with the money instead.

Later that afternoon, what was left of Lily's nail varnish disappeared when she 'helped' her mum at the allotment, getting herself covered in mud and twigs. Kara's tomato plants had gone mad and had almost reached the top of their support canes, but she tied them in the best she could and removed any side shoots to ensure energy went into tomato production. There were several trusses of small yellow flowers and Kara was pleased to see that a few had already started to grow into tiny green tomatoes.

Gathering the redundant side shoots up, she held them up to her nose for a moment, breathing in the wonderful green aroma unique to growing tomatoes. The smell took her immediately back to being Lily's age, helping her dad on the allotment. He always gave her the very first ripe tomato to eat, presenting it to her with a flourish. Kara remembered the sweet taste, the juice running down her chin, and her dad smiling happily at her. Dumping the shoots in her compost bin, Kara spied Zoe and Ben on their allotment and went to say hello, leaving Lily to play happily within her sight. Zoe howled when she told them about their morning's entertainment, but then looked pensive.

"I wonder who she is meeting that's so important?" she asked turning to Ben.

"Let's have a look, shall we?" said Ben, pulling out his phone.

"What!" exclaimed Kara.

"Ben put in a couple of security cameras for Josie," replied Zoe in a matter-of-fact voice. "He was just checking they were working a couple of weeks ago, and, well, there was some very interesting footage. It's probably completely illegal but we've been downloading the footage ever since."

"Hmm, that's interesting," said Ben. "Not Smythe this time, but one of those men we saw walking around with him a few weeks ago."

"What!" exclaimed Kara, again.

"Poppy 'entertains' men in the barn in the afternoons, Kara," said Zoe.

"Might they just be business meetings?" asked Kara.

"Certainly, the oldest business in the world," replied Zoe.

"But how do you know that?" asked Kara. "Surely all you see are them entering the barn?"

"Ah well, that's the bit that might be more illegal than the rest," replied Ben, looking a tiny bit shamefaced. "I put in a camera to see through the top windows. And a microphone."

Kara stared at him, then checked Lily was still playing happily before holding out her hand for the phone.

"Show me," she said.

Kara watched the video footage open-mouthed but didn't get to the end of it as Lily fell over and came running over in tears. She quickly thrust the phone back at Ben as she didn't want a nosy Lily to see what she was had just seen.

"I'll call you later," she said, given him a dark look as she rubbed Lily's knee better, before taking her to visit Dorothy.

Jack had arranged for extra carer visits for Dorothy whilst he was away, but Kara had also promised to drop in every day to check on her. Dorothy loved seeing Lily and was happily engaged cuddled up on the sofa sharing a picture story book with her, which freed up Kara's mind to think about what she had seen on Ben's phone. She almost wished she hadn't seen it, as it would be very difficult to shake the images from her mind.

The high up camera gave a direct line of sight straight through one window to a mattress covered in red shiny material. You couldn't see what the mattress was standing on as the fabric draped to the floor, but possibly pallets, or whatever was in the barn already, as it was unlikely that Poppy could have got a bed base through the woods and into the barn – even a mattress would have taken some doing.

In the footage of when Smythe visited her, Poppy was dressed in a black leather dominatrix outfit, complete with spike heeled thigh boots and a whip. In the bit of footage Kara saw he was kneeling on all fours with a dog lead around his neck whilst Poppy straddled him and smacked his bottom. Kara would have been disgusted if it hadn't been so funny, the overbearing Smythe submitting to the assault meekly whilst admitting that he was a 'naughty boy'. His scrawny white body almost glowed in the dim light, a contrast with the long black socks and highly polished shoes he had left on. Poppy's flesh bulged out of the tight outfit, and Kara couldn't help thinking that Smythe would need to visit a physio after having her weight on his back.

Later, once Lily was in bed, she called Ben and Zoe to talk about the footage.

"I'm not sure you should be keeping this Ben," she said. "What goes on behind closed doors is their own business, surely?"

"Yes and no, Kara," replied Ben, "What's going on in there could be very much our business."

"What do you mean?" asked Kara.

"Well, I couldn't hear everything – the microphone picking up through the glass is very muffled – but Poppy and Smythe are clearly cooking up some deal to do with planning permission and are intending to split a big bribe fifty/fifty," he replied.

"Okay. That's illegal, but I'm not sure how it affects us," replied Kara.

"Neither was I," replied Ben, "but the man who visited today was one of the men that were walking around the allotments with Smythe and Gilbert. There wasn't much talking, as he was gagged and tied up whilst she 'administered' to him, but as he left, he looked at the view over the allotments and I clearly heard him say that the view would be a great selling point."

"That doesn't sound good, Ben," replied Kara. "I think you'd better keep recording to see what they're up to, but don't tell Josie, she would be horrified!"

# CHAPTER FORTY-FIVE

The allotments were at their best, verdant with foliage and ripe with plump fruit and vegetables. The new paths had inspired several of the allotment holders to tidy up their plots, give old sheds a lick of green paint and get rid of rubbish. A heavy shower had washed away all the dust of construction, and the plants, refreshed, raised their faces to the sun.

Mary's Memorial Allotment was finished and ready, with wide level paths and wheelchair accessible raised beds filled with new soil that was easy to plant in without having to dig it over first. There was a wheelchair-height long table under a blue awning that could be used as a potting bench or a place where wheelchair users could gather to chat. Ben and Jack's shed had wide doors and racks to hold tools at wheelchair height, but also plenty of space to come in out of the rain and make a hot drink. The garden could accommodate four disabled gardeners: at present all beds were empty and waiting, but David had put his name down for one and there had already been several enquiries for the others.

The sensory and children's garden had been planted up with lavender, rosemary and other fragrant herbs, with thyme planted in gaps in the path so that it would release its scent when walked upon. Foxgloves, echinacea, verbena and delphinium gave splashes of bright colour and attracted bees and butterflies. Feathery grasses and plants with soft spikes were planted where you would brush against them when passing. A bench dedicated to Mary (with the inscription also in braille) was surrounded by the delicate grasses so you could hear the wind move through them and run your fingers through them whilst seated.

The elephant water feature was fitted with a recirculating pump powered by a hidden solar panel and its shiny mosaic tiles glinted in the sun. The sound of splashing water from its trunk mixed with the hum of bees and lilting bird song as birds flocked to the many birdfeeders hung all around the garden. A child-height raised bed was ready for little gardeners with a brightly coloured mud kitchen adding fun. Bobbie's hanging cocoon seat was in place and Kara had made all-weather cushions in bright colours for it; Jack couldn't wait for Bobby to see it.

The school's visit to Disneyland Paris had been a great success, but looking after Bobby full time had been exhausting, especially as, despite not liking loud noises and bright lights, he loved rollercoasters. Jack wasn't a big fan, but as Bobby's designated carer, he had to go on the rides with him. They would just get off one and before Jack had got his breath back, Bobby had already dashed on to the next one, a green-faced Jake trying to keep him in sight.

Jack was very glad to be home, especially as he had missed Kara a great deal, but found that he was actually missing Bobby a little now that the school holidays had started. He had come to understand more of how Bobby's extraordinary brain worked and how you needed to work with him and not try and make him conform to 'normal' behaviour. Jack hoped to finish the Level 3 Diploma in 'Supporting Teaching and Learning' over the holidays and was seriously thinking of going on afterwards to take additional courses, focusing on working with children on the autism spectrum, and maybe after that take a teaching degree.

It had been decided to wait to have a formal opening of Mary's Memorial Allotment in the early autumn, as soon as the schools were back, so that all the children could also come to see 'their' garden. It would be timed to coincide with the annual produce show and be a full day of events; the small delay would give them time to plan it and for the new gardens to become more established.

Jack hoped they would have an Indian summer, with days of warm golden sunshine for the event. He remembered the frustration he had felt as a small boy being back at school and confined inside whilst the sun was streaming through the tall windows, roasting him in his itchy new school uniform. He realised that even then he was never happier than when he was outside and reflected that even though he'd been in a bad place when he was homeless, being outside had been a balm to his soul.

With six weeks of school holiday, and a full order book of gardening jobs, Jack was happy that he was going to be outside most of the summer; but first he had Dorothy's hundredth birthday party to plan. Jack glanced at his watch and saw he just had time to buy some flowers for Josie before he and Kara went to see her to plan the party. It was good to have a regular income now and be able to buy flowers, treat Kara to a meal out occasionally, or get a small toy for the children.

Josie hadn't been out and about since she'd sprained her ankle and Kara was worried about her, especially as she had sounded very down when Kara had phoned her. As well as Jack's flowers, Kara had made Josie some of her famous brownies to cheer her up but was shocked when she saw Josie's pale drawn face at the door.

"Can you make us all some tea, Jack," said Kara, winking at Jack to try and convey she wanted a woman-to-woman chat with Josie, before she followed Josie as she hobbled through to the garden.

"Are you in a lot of pain, Josie?" Kara asked once they were settled under the apple tree in the shade with Josie's foot up on a padded box.

"It's not too bad now, thank you Kara," said Josie with a small smile, "as long as I don't stand on it for too long. The allotment is a bit far though just yet, which is a shame as I'd love to see the finished memorial garden."

"Well, it is fully accessible you know now," said Kara with a grin, "so how about I borrow a wheelchair from work this afternoon and we go and visit?"

"On no, I couldn't put you through all that trouble," replied Josie looking flustered.

"It's no trouble, and we could do with someone to road test the new paths!" replied Kara with a laugh. She quickly stopped laughing when she saw tears starting to fall down Josie's face. Josie was the most capable, together person she knew, and to see her upset was a shock.

"Whatever is the matter, Josie?" she said, putting her arms around her.

"I'm so sorry Kara, ignore me – I'm just being silly," said Josie.

"No, you're not. You're in pain and probably haven't been sleeping and everything seems worse when you haven't had enough sleep."

Josie fished in her pocket for a tissue and blew her nose.

"You're right, I'm finding it difficult to get comfortable in bed. It's not just my ankle, but my shoulder hurts when I lay on it too and I've been spending most of the night sat up."

"No wonder you're feeling emotional, Josie. If I have just one bad night, I'm horrible all day!"

"I can vouch for that," said Jack, putting the tray down and handing Josie a cup of tea.

"Oi you, less of that!" said Kara, giving Jack a playful slap on his bottom.

"See that, Josie! Sexual harassment!" said Jack.

"I think that's what's really upsetting me," said Josie.

"What, someone's been sexually harassing you?" said Kara, outraged.

"No, no – of course not. But, having been stuck at home all week I realise I miss it."

"What, sex?" asked Kara, her mouth falling open.

"No, no, not sex… exactly, but a partner. Someone to talk to, someone to look after me when I'm unwell, someone to give me a hug. I'm usually so busy, out and about, at the allotment, the church, the WI and the school, and being so long on my own has made me realise that I'm lonely."

"Oh Josie, I'm so sorry," said Kara, giving her another hug.

Jack put his arms around both of them, and they stayed like that for a while in the sun filled garden as birdsong washed over them like a blessing.

"Okay," said Josie, blowing her nose and taking a sip of tea. "Enough of me feeling sorry for myself. We have a birthday party to arrange!"

"That's more like the Josie I know!" said Kara, handing her a brownie.

Jack realised that Josie needed to be kept busy to take her mind off things, and he had just the job for her, one that she could do sitting down and that would suit her talent as a detective.

"I need your help, Josie," he said. "Kara and I can organise food and drink, and Zoe's organising local celebrations via Facebook, but we don't know of anyone in Dorothy's family to invite. She says I'm her only living relative, but that can't be true. It would mean so much to her to have other relatives there."

"Hmm," said Josie, brightening up. "I'm a member of *Ancestry.com*, so I could do a search via that, but, well, we could play her at her own game and do a DNA relative search too!

"Great idea!" said Jack. "I'll sneak a DNA sample and you can do the rest!

When the couple left half an hour later, Josie was looking much brighter, but Jack couldn't help worrying about her. He knew that Kara was the love of his life, and if Josie had had that with Keith, he dreaded to think what she must feel like without him now.

# CHAPTER FORTY-SIX

There was a small garden between the manor and the allotments which consisted of a wide lawn surrounded by herbaceous borders, the last remaining piece of the manor's once extensive formal gardens. Jack had worked hard to ensure that the somewhat neglected boarders were a riot of colour in time for Dorothy's birthday, and after a final tidy-up, he stood back in satisfaction to admire them and the small marquee that he and Ben had erected on the lawn the day before.

Kara and Zoe had worked their magic on the plain marquee, with swags of multi-coloured flags, ribbons and hundreds of fairy lights, and Josie had added great tubs of flowers. A large banner wishing Dorothy a 'Happy 100th Birthday' was hung across the entrance, and as many comfortable chairs as they could beg, borrow or steal were inside, with little tables (some just fruit boxes with a cloth over them) next to each one to place drinks or plates of food. The outside 'gardener's' toilet had been spruced up with a good clean, a coat of paint, a vase of flowers and nice soap and towels, with a jaunty little sign on the path pointing the way.

In case of rain, the manor's impressive entrance hall was also decked out with flags and flowers, but thankfully it was a lovely golden summers day, so the hall would only be used for serving food and drink. All the local food shops had donated food – pies, cakes, freshly baked bread, baskets of fruit and bowls of sweets for the children – and these were beautifully arranged on the cloth covered trestle tables borrowed from the village hall. Each of the three local pubs had donated barrels of beer or a case or two of wine, and the local hotel had supplied crockery, glasses and waiting staff.

Dorothy had been kept in the dark about the preparation, with the curtains closed and everyone sworn to silence, so when she stepped into the hall on Jack's arm, she gave a cry of astonishment at seeing the hall full of food and drink.

"This all looks lovely Jack," she said, "but we are never going to able to eat all this!"

"Oh, I think we may have a little help," replied Jack, grinning as he guided her slowly out into the sunshine, where the local boy scouts were lined up in a guard of honour from the front door to the marquee.

The town's Silver Band stuck up 'Happy Birthday', and for a terrible moment Jack thought they'd got it all wrong, as Dorothy stopped and put her hand to her chest. He just hoped it wasn't all too much for her, but then she turned to him, her eyes shining, and kissed his cheek.

"Thank you, Jack, this is wonderful," she said, before standing up straight and waving to everyone as she made her way regally to the marquee.

Although there was only room in the marquee for invited guests, the whole town appeared to have turned up to celebrate 'their' Lady's century, and the road outside was packed. Fortunately, Josie had thought about this and had got a road closure notice in place, so there was room for everyone to gather safely and a street party was in full swing with several food stalls and a bouncy castle. The Council had joined in the celebration and had slung flags from lamppost to lamppost back and forth across the road and they fluttered in the sunshine creating a festive feeling.

Josie recognised the yellow and blue flags were from when the Tour de Yorkshire cycling race came through Kirkby a couple of years before and smiled, remembering another great community event. It was days like this that made her proud to be a Yorkshire woman and especially proud of the open-hearted people of Kirkby. The malaise that had afflicted her of late lifted as she looked around at her friends and neighbours, many of whom greeted her with a smile, a wave or a warm hug.

Inside the marquee Dorothy was sitting in state whilst guest after guest came up to wish her happy birthday. Many of them she knew from the various local organisations that she was the patron of, and she was very pleased to see them and hear their news. However, to her astonishment and pleasure, one by one, Josie introduced her to distant family members, all descended from her grandparent's siblings and children. There was a clear family resemblance, and when they all gathered around Dorothy for a group photograph, there was no doubt they were family.

The band, who were on the balcony of the penthouse apartment, were now playing a medley of war-time songs, and whilst Dorothy was the oldest person there, there were several elderly guests who knew all the words and were singing along. Then the music changed to a single trumpet and a soldier, immaculate in the uniform of Henry's old regiment, marched into the marquee, stopped in front of Dorothy, stood to attention and saluted. Dorothy knew from his pips that he was a major, the same rank as her father had been, and she resisted the urge to salute back as she used to do in fun to her father.

"Lady Kirkby, your fiancé Captain Henry Neville was awarded the Victoria Cross for valour in the presence of the enemy. The award was never sent to his family, and, at the request of Captain Neville's great-grandson, it is my great honour to present it to you in his memory."

Dorothy gasped, tears running down her face as the major held a slim box towards her. Her hands were shaking too much to take it, so Jack stepped forward, took the box and lifted out the shining medal on its cerise ribbon and pinned it to her dress. The major saluted again, and everyone applauded long and loud, with cheers from the neighbours outside raising above the sound as the news was passed from person to person.

Just as it started to quieten down, the trumpet sounded again and everyone turned expectantly towards the entrance of the marquee. Lily stood there uncertainly in her best dress, a posy in one hand and an envelope in the other.

"Go on," stage-whispered Kara, and everyone smiled.

After another moment's hesitation, Lily shyly walked towards Dorothy, bobbed her the curtsey she had been practising and handed her the envelope.

"This is from the Queen," she said, "and this is from me," she added, thrusting the posy at Dorothy, before running to hide behind Kara, suddenly overcome.

There was laughter and more clapping, and people gathered around Dorothy to congratulate her and look at the Queen's birthday message and Henry's medal. Lily was also the centre of attention and her shyness was soon forgotten as she basked in the praise heaped upon her. Eventually, people started to drift towards the food and drink and the party then continued on into the evening, well after Dorothy had retired, happy but worn out with the day's events.

# AUTUMN

# CHAPTER FORTY-SEVEN

There was a bumper crop of apples from the little orchard that bordered the allotments and Kara, Jack and Josie were working together to peel, core and freeze as many apples as they could all get in their freezers. Trays of apples had been stored in allotment holder's sheds and garages, with bags of surplus apples left at the allotments gates for local residents to help themselves to. Any apples still left over were given to the local environmental group who had an apple press going, making gallons of apple juice from the town's surplus which raised funds for local charities.

"I love it that nothing goes to waste," said Josie, busy peeling apples before passing them to Jack to chop prior to Kara packing them and getting them into the freezer before they turned brown.

"We'll be eating apple pie for months!" said Kara.

"Yummy!" replied Jack with a grin.

Whilst they worked, they discussed the upcoming official opening of the Memorial Allotment and the Annual Produce Show.

"Who shall we get to open it?" asked Josie.

"Well, I asked Great-Grandma," replied Jack, "but she says she is still recovering from her birthday party and asks if she can kindly pass on the honour this year."

"Is she all right, Jack?" asked Josie.

"She's as well as a 100-year-old can be, but, much as she loved her party, it did take it out of her," replied Jack.

"Probably all that champagne she drank!" said Kara. "I know it took me a few days to get over it."

"It was a wonderful day, wasn't it?" asked Josie, and everyone agreed.

"So, our 'Grand Opening' and Annual Produce Show can't compete, but it would be good to make it just as special if we can," Josie continued.

It was agreed that they would ask the Lord Mayor to open Mary's Memorial Allotment, but other than that, it would be a very child-focused event to foster the next generation of gardeners. It was decided that a local schoolchild, picked at random, would open the children's garden. Josie told them she was going to sponsor a new class at the produce show for all local children to enter any allotment or home-grown vegetables. To ensure that children without access to a garden didn't get left out, Kara offered to sponsor a competition for the best painting of a garden, a vegetable or a flower.

"Some music would be nice," said Jack, and found he had volunteered to get the school choir ready to perform at the event.

Zoe was volunteered in her absence to publicise the event, and John, as usual, would be asked to ensure that the prize money for the hotly fought over best flower and vegetable categories was all ready to be presented. Josie offered to get all the annual trophies back from the previous year's winners to get them cleaned ready to be re-presented.

"Although there seems little point getting the biggest marrow trophy back from John," she said, "as he's bound to win it again. I don't know what he feeds that thing, but it's enormous!"

Jack, who hadn't experienced the annual produce show before, was then regaled with stories from previous years of the disputes, sabotage and near fights over the various best vegetable categories.

"It's not the prize money," explained Josie, "but the pride of winning the major awards. For some allotment holders, it's been three generations of winning 'best dahlia' or 'most perfect carrots', and it's almost a religion!"

"I wouldn't be surprised if John camped out overnight to protect his marrow!" said Kara with a laugh.

Jack, knowing how cold and uncomfortable that would be, decided to have a word with Ben about a CCTV 'marrow cams' so that John could sleep in his own bed with peace of mind.

# CHAPTER FORTY-EIGHT

With no one to come home to, John spent more time at the allotment and as the annual produce show approached, some might say that he was guarding his marrow in the hope of winning the 'biggest marrow' trophy for the sixth year running. There was a grain of truth in that, as he was pretty sure that his marrows were the biggest he had ever grown, and sabotage by a rival grower was not unheard of, but he was also enjoying spending time with David and Hugo who were busy getting David's allotment started.

There was a lot to do at this time of year, harvesting crops and preparing the soil for the following year. John had already lifted his potatoes and onions and had put them into storage, the potatoes at the back of his garage behind a hanging tarpaulin to keep them in the dark and the onions in neat bunches hanging from the roof in his allotment shed where they would get plenty of light.

He had been picking his late season strawberries and raspberries daily and harvesting his courgettes and outdoor tomatoes every few days, putting his surplus produce on the swap bench or giving it to Kara for the local food bank.

His pear tree, planted many years ago by Mary, had cropped well this year, and looking at its laden branches, John's eyes had filled with tears when he thought how pleased she would have been. In previous years she would have made any surplus into pear chutney, and with only one precious jar left, he decided he would give Mary's recipe and a big bag of pears to Josie, in the hope she would give him back some jars of chutney to have in the evenings with his cheese and biscuit suppers.

John's task today was to dig up and compost all the plants that had finished their season, sow hardy winter lettuce and spinach, then plant out his spring cabbage seedlings. He arrived early, eager to make a start whilst the weather held, and was surprised to see Poppy Gilbert just about to enter his plot.

"Can I help you Ms Gilbert?" he said, making her jump as she hadn't heard him approach.

"No, no, I'm fine," she replied, putting her hands behind her back, but not before John caught the glint of a knife.

"I, er, thought I saw a stray cat came in here and didn't want it to damage your marrows," Poppy said as she backed out.

John's eyebrows shot up and he went straight to check on his, hopefully, prizewinning marrows. Thankfully, they were untouched, nestling happily on their bed of straw, looking magnificent. There was no sign of any cats, but by the time he turned around, Poppy was gone. As he worked on his garden, he wondered how she had known about his marrow as it was not visible from the path. A suspicion began to form in his mind and when a female voice called out "Hello," he snapped back angrily "What do you want?" without looking up, thinking it was Poppy returning.

"Oh, I'm sorry to disturb you," the woman replied, and John looked up, before lowering his gaze to a lady with neatly bobbed grey hair in a wheelchair outside the entrance to his allotment.

"I'm so sorry," replied John, "I thought you were someone else. How can I help you?"

"Well, I'm glad I'm not whoever else you thought I was," she said, with a raised eyebrow and the hint of a grin. "Could you point me in the direction of the accessible allotments, please. I wanted to have a look at them and check they were truly accessible before I put my name down for one."

"Let me show you the way," said John, eager to make up for his rudeness.

"You're very kind," she replied, before following him along the path.

David was already at the accessible allotments and wheeled straight over to say hello.

"Hi, you must be Sarah," he said shaking her hand.

"Yes, and you must be David," she replied.

"I see you have met John already," said David.

"Well, sort of. He kindly showed me the way here," said Sarah.

"John is very kind. It was his idea to build the accessible allotments, in memory of his late wife," replied David.

"Oh!" said Sarah, giving John an empathetic look. "I'm sorry for your loss, John."

John just nodded, unable to speak without a break in his voice, a problem he encountered whenever Mary was mentioned.

"Sarah got in touch with me about the allotment on our accessibility group Facebook page," explained David, sensing he had inadvertently upset John and wanting to move onto safer ground.

"Yes," said Sarah. "And you did not exaggerate. This is perfect. Can I put my name down for one?"

"You certainly can," said John.

Sarah thanked him with a smile that reminded him so much of Mary's bright smile that he had to turn away, and with a gruff 'I'll leave you to it' he headed back to the safety of his own allotment.

As he worked, he wondered what Sarah's story was; whether she had always been a wheelchair user or had had an accident or a health issue that more recently affected her mobility. She looked nothing like Mary apart for when she smiled, but was probably a similar age, and John knew that if the worst that had befallen Mary was being confined to a wheelchair, he would have been grateful.

# CHAPTER FORTY-NINE

Whilst Mary's Memorial Allotment and the children's garden were being officially opened by the Lord Mayor, judging of the entries for the produce show was taking place behind closed doors in the Town Hall. The judges came from other allotments or horticultural societies, all specialist in one category or another and took their task seriously, weighing, measuring and examining the flowers and vegetables from every angle.

The judge of the children's vegetables was the Kirkby school headmaster, and the judge of the children's paintings was the art lecturer from the local Sixth Form College. They were less exacting in their decision making, but the quality of what the children had produced still made it difficult to pick out the winners.

One category, that gave all allotment holders who didn't want to concentrate on just one specific vegetable a chance of a major prize, was 'a basket of vegetables'. This was sponsored by the local greengrocers and had a prize of £200 attached, so it was a very popular category, especially as every vegetable didn't have to be perfect, just good quality across the whole basket and nicely displayed.

Growers could choose which five different vegetables to include, so every basket was different and it was usually difficult to judge, but this year there was a clear winner, as each individual vegetable was perhaps more perfect that those that had been entered for species specific categories. Josie and Kara, who had dashed down to the town hall to get the tea urn on before the dignitaries arrived for refreshments, stared at the First Prize certificate in astonishment.

"Poppy Gilbert!" exclaimed Kara.

"Well, I never realised she was such a good grower," said Josie, equally surprised but trying not to show it.

"Neither did I," replied Kara. "She never seemed to spend any time on her vegetable beds. Other kinds of beds, well, that's a different story..."

Josie shot her a look, but as allotment holders, eager to see if they had won anything, were starting to rush into the hall, she made her way to the refreshment room ready to hand out tea and cakes. John came in a few moments later, beaming from ear to ear and Josie didn't have to ask him if his giant marrow had won as that was obvious.

"Four centimetres bigger than last year!" boasted John proudly.

"Now what is it you're talking about?" said Sarah, who had just wheeled herself into the room. She waggled her eyebrows suggestively and John blushed, making Sarah laugh.

Josie looked from one to the other as John carried tea and cake for two to a table and Sarah joined him, touching his arm in thanks. For the first time in ages, John looked relaxed and happy and whilst Josie was happy that he had made a new friend, she couldn't help feeling a stab of jealousy. Despite being surrounded by many friends and acquaintances, she felt very alone all of a sudden. Feeling her eyes well up, she made a dash to the loo to do some deep breathing and give herself a good talking to.

She locked the cubical door and sat on the toilet lid whilst she fished in her bag for her bottle of rescue remedy and a tissue. The longer she stayed there, the less inclined she felt to return to the crowded hall: for once the Allotment Association would have to manage without their Chair. She heard the door open and hoped it wasn't Kara coming to find her as she was likely to burst into tears if Kara was kind to her. Josie was relieved when she recognised the grating voice of the Lady Mayoress and then the timid voice of Mrs Smythe, who had attended in her husband's unexplained absence.

The Lady Mayoress was enthusing about the accessible allotments and the sensory garden, and Mrs Smythe appeared to have enjoyed seeing the children having fun in their own garden. The hand dryer blasted out and drowned out Mrs Smythe's next comment, but the Lady Mayoress loud voice cut across it.

"Are you sure, Joan? The allotments will be closing?" she cried.

The reply was inaudible, but then Josie clearly heard the Lady Mayoress's response agreeing that, "Well, yes, the town does need more housing" before the door banged shut behind them.

Josie was shocked, her own problem's forgotten, and she dashed back into the hall intent on confronting Mrs Smythe to find out the truth. She was met by a commotion as Tom, a veteran allotment holder, was angrily confronting a smug Poppy Gilbert, who was holding her trophy and an envelope containing her winnings.

"That's my squash in your basket," said Tom.

"You're only jealous because I won and you didn't!" said Poppy, hand on her hips, grinning as she tucked the envelope provocatively into her overflowing bra and tossed the trophy from hand to hand.

A circle had formed around them and Josie, who had more important things to deal with, tried to get past without being dragged into whatever was going on but had no luck, as Tom saw her and appealed to her.

"Josie! You know that no one else grows Rugosa Friulana squash. I brought them there seeds back from Italy when I visited my daughter last year. You remember me telling you?

Josie did remember and peered into Poppy's basket where the pale warty squash had pride of place. She remembered Tom telling her in great detail about his holiday and the flavoursome but unattractive squash he had eaten and would try to grow himself.

"Poppy, would you pass me the Rugosa Friulana please?" she said, holding out her hand.

Poppy looked down at the basket, an uncertain look on her face and then picked up a very dark green courgette and dropped it into Josie's hand.

"No Ms Gilbert. That's a 'Black Beauty' courgette if I'm not mistaken. Do you want a second attempt?" she asked sweetly.

The crowd started to snigger, and Poppy flushed red, before dropping the basket and pushing past Josie and out of the door, still clutching the trophy and with the money, presumably, still within her ample cleavage.

"Don't worry, Tom, it's a cheque, we'll get it stopped and then do a full investigation," said Josie, rubbing her shoulder that had only just recovered from Poppy's last assault and felt like it was going to be sore again.

Other allotment holders stepped forward and picked up the fallen vegetables, claiming that they were their best specimens that had gone missing from their allotments, so it was a few moments before Kara could get away. She frantically scanned the room, but it was too late: Mrs Smythe and the Lady Mayoress had gone.

A few minutes later Jack arrived, having remained at the allotments until all the children had left. He was feeling very happy as the children's garden was a big success and Bobby had loved his hanging cocoon seat. He was especially happy as he had received the decree absolute that morning and was now free to marry Kara. He was racking his brain for a romantic way to properly propose to her, when Josie grabbed his arm and pulled him into the empty kitchen.

Josie's face was ashen, and she looked close to tears, so giving her a moment to compose herself, Jack went to find her a cup of tea whilst signalling to Kara to join them. Kara, thinking Josie wanted to speak to them about Poppy Gilberts most recent 'crime', started to talk about it as soon as she entered the kitchen.

"Can you believe the cheek of the woman? Stealing people's best vegetables and passing them off as her own?" Kara said indignantly.

"What?" exclaimed Jack who had missed all the commotion.

"Well…" started Kara, but was silenced by Josie, holding up her hand for quiet in the way that Kara remembered from her days at school.

"The allotments are going to close," said Josie quietly.

"What?" exclaimed Jack again, all the joy of the day draining out of him.

"I overheard bits of a conversation between Mrs Smythe and the Lady Mayoress," explained Josie. "Something about it being a pity the allotments would be closed, and the need for local housing."

Jack and Josie stared at her open mouthed.

"Are you sure Josie?" asked Kara.

"No. I could be putting two and two together and making five, but that is what I heard. I tried to catch Mrs Smythe to find out more, but she was gone," replied Josie wearily, absentmindedly rubbing her shoulder.

"Okay," said Jack. "Let's not panic. We need to find out what's going on. I'll find John, Ben and Zoe and get them to meet with us later this afternoon, as soon as the show's finished. It's a pity Hugo's on holiday, as he would know the planning process from his days of being a local house builder, but let's make a start and put together a plan of action."

The other two nodded, and whilst Jack went in search of the others, Kara remained with Josie who she could see was upset. Before they could talk, someone came into the kitchen looking for Josie and she took a deep breath, put on her professional face and went to sort out whatever it was. No one seeing her calm authority would have guessed at the turmoil going on inside.

# CHAPTER FIFTY

They all met at Josie's a couple of hours later. Ben, Zoe and John all presumed that the meeting was about the 'Stolen Vegetable Scandal', and Zoe was already planning a Facebook exposé, so they were deeply shocked when Josie told them what she had overheard. There was a moment's silence and then everyone spoke at once, outrage, disbelief and distress spilling out. After a few moments mayhem, Jack's voice cut across the noise.

"Okay, we need a plan. First things first, we need to check the facts. Anyone know how to do that?" he asked.

"Well, they would need planning permission, so I guess we start with the council's planning website," said Zoe, her fingers already busy on her phone.

"When we put up an annex on the school, it was in the newspaper and notices were affixed to lamp posts around the area: I've not seen anything, so presumably the planning application hasn't been put in yet?

"Found it!" exclaimed Zoe. "An application for thirty 'executive homes' on the site of the 'former allotments' has been registered. All are detached and have five or six bedrooms and double garages – just what Kirkby needs – not! Hang on: according to the timeline, it has already been out of local resident's consultation with no objections received!"

"What?" exclaimed Kara. "That's not true!"

"'Former allotments indeed!" spluttered John.

"There is a date for the next meeting of the Planning Committee here," said Zoe, still scrolling on her phone. "The application will be heard then."

"When is it?" asked Josie quietly.

"Two weeks' time!" replied Zoe.

"It's too late then," replied Josie, putting her head in her hands.

Kara shot Jack a look and then put her arm around Josie, almost as worried about her depressed state of mind as she was about the sale of the allotments.

"It's not too late, Josie," said Jack quietly. "Two weeks is plenty of time if rules are being broken: we just need the evidence."

"There is the video…" said Ben uncertainly.

"What video?" asked Josie.

"Promise you won't be cross?" replied Zoe.

"Just show them it, Zoe!" said Kara.

"Are you sure?" asked Zoe, glancing at John and then Josie and then raising her eyebrows at Kara. "It's a bit X-rated…"

"I'm sure it's nothing we haven't seen before," replied John.

"I wouldn't be so sure about that!" muttered Zoe.

They all crammed into Josie's little sitting room and Ben connected his phone to Josie's TV and then pressed play. When the video finished, there was a shocked silence.

"I've obviously lived a very sheltered life!" muttered Josie eventually.

"That is disgusting!" exploded John. "On Allotment Association property as well. They are breaking at least three of the Allotment Rules."

Kara burst out laughing, breaking the tension in the room.

"Oh John!" she said, shaking her head and smiling at him fondly. "Only you would say that at a time like this!"

She glanced at Jack to share a smile and was surprised to see he wasn't taking any notice but was slowly winding the video back.

"Jack!" she exclaimed. "I'm surprised at you. I wouldn't have thought you'd be the type to want to re-watch porn on slo-mo!"

Jack stopped the video on the frame that showed the man that Poppy had entertained surveying the view across the allotments. Jack stared at him intently.

"Ben, can you make that any clearer, please?" he asked.

"Yes, think so. Once I get home, I can isolate the frame as a still shot and then I should be able to enhance it."

"Why Jack, what is it?" asked Zoe.

"I'm not sure, but I think I might know that man," replied Jack.

"Really?" asked Kara. "Where from?"

"Well, as you know, in my old life, I was an accountant," he began.

"You, an accountant!" interrupted Zoe. "No way can I see you stuck in an office all day."

"I know," replied Jack with a small smile, "I always hated it – I just longed to be outside. But anyway, I was, for far too many years."

"And?" prompted Kara.

"Well, he looks like a former client," replied Jack. "If it's who I think it is, I did a large piece of work for them, sorting out the finances of a company they had just acquired – a building company called Hawk Developments. It was a right mess, and I worked some long hours, so when I'd finished, him and his wife took me and my ex-wife out for a meal."

"Your ex-wife?" queried Kara.

"Yes, my love. I haven't had the chance to tell you yet, but I got the final divorce papers this morning. I'm now a free man!"

Kara threw her arms around him, and they hugged for a moment, almost forgetting the others, until John cleared his throat loudly.

"And how does that help us, Jack?" he asked.

"Blackmail!" said Zoe, excitedly. "We could blackmail him about his liaison with Gilbert!"

"No!" Jack and Josie exclaimed together.

"We don't stoop as low as them, Zoe," said Josie in her best Headmistress voice.

"Well, I reckon I owe him a drink," said Jack, "and I happen to know which local he uses and that he does like a drink or ten. Maybe I could get some info out of him over a G&T, something that would give us an edge? So, if it is him, do you fancy a trip to Leeds, Kara, to celebrate my divorce?"

"Oh yes: as long as I can shop too!" Kara replied, giving him another hug.

"Hmm, still think blackmail would be easier!" said Zoe huffily.

"No!" they all chorused.

"Did you say that the company your acquaintance took over was called Hawk Developments?" asked Josie suddenly.

"Yes, why?" replied Jack.

"Well, a few weeks ago there was a company surveying the road outside allotments. They had a logo on their hi-vis jackets, a bird of some kind. It may well have been a hawk."

"Sounds like we are getting somewhere," said Ben. "Do you think Friday night would be the best chance to catch this man in the pub, Jack?

Jack nodded, and Ben continued.

"Okay, so we all need to be finding out what we can in the meantime. John, Josie if you can see what you can find out from any council contacts, Zoe and I will see what we can find out online."

That agreed, they moved on to talk briefly about Poppy's alleged theft of prize vegetables. Jack had missed all the excitement and was shocked at Poppy's barefaced cheek.

"There is no way she grew those vegetables," he said, "because nothing but weeds is growing on her allotment!"

"Could she have grown them somewhere else?" asked Josie, trying to be fair.

"I doubt it, as she only has a small flat with no garden," said Kara.

"Have we checked the marrow-cam, Ben?" asked Zoe, turning towards him.

"The marrow-cam?" asked Josie, eyebrows shooting up.

"Oh yes," replied John nonchalantly. "Ben kindly put a hidden camera on my allotment to cover my marrows after I saw Gilbert sneaking around early one morning with a knife. I'm very grateful, as I'd have been having sleepless nights otherwise."

Josie put her head in her hands.

"I dread to think how many laws we've been breaking with all these hidden cameras!" she said.

"Not as many as Gilbert has been," replied Ben, as he accessed the marrow-cam footage on his phone.

"Hmm. The camera I set up for you, John, shows a little of Tom's allotment and a bit of Hugo's in the background. Its only at low level, but there is someone entering both allotments early this morning. I'm pretty sure those thunder thighs are Gilbert's, but I'll see if I can get it any clearer when I enhance that other section for Jack."

"I'll go and have a look at Hugo's allotment and see if any of his veg has been recently removed," said John. "With him being away, there shouldn't be any fresh cuts on stalks."

It was agreed that John would stop the cheque and that Josie would write to Poppy telling her that her allotment membership was suspended pending a full investigation. They arranged to meet up again the following Saturday once Jack and Kara were back from Leeds, and then everyone bid Josie goodnight before they went their separate ways.

Josie stood for a while in the doorway, looking out over her garden, rubbing her tender shoulder absentmindedly and thinking about the events of the day. It seemed very quiet now everyone had gone and she felt very alone: it would have been nice to have someone's arms around her, to sit together in the golden evening with a glass of wine and discuss what had happened, maybe laugh a little, finding the ridiculous in the shocking video.

She watched a sunlit bee bumble from flower to flower, nonchalantly avoiding Lucky who suddenly appeared from the undergrowth and leaped at it, before rubbing herself against Josie's legs, purring and meowing for her dinner. Josie bent and stroked her, then picked her up, holding her soft body against her chest for a moment before heading inside, glad someone needed her, even if it was just a cat.

# CHAPTER FIFTY-ONE

Josie tossed and turned for ages, mulling things over, before falling into a deep sleep. She was awoken by the phone ringing, and glancing at her clock, surprised to see it was after nine. Groggily she picked up the phone and was soon wide awake as she listened to John raging about a letter he had just received from Smythe.

"The cheek of the man. Evicted indeed!" he seethed.

"What are you talking about John?" asked Josie, as she plodded downstairs and tried to fill the kettle for a much needed cup of tea without dropping the phone.

"The letter says I've been evicted from my allotment for non-payment of invoices!" spluttered John. "I'm the Treasurer and never in my life have I been in debt. How dare he?"

"Hang on John, the post lady is just here. I'll see if I've got one too," said Josie.

Sure enough, there was a brown envelope baring the Council's frank mark and Josie tore it open to reveal that she had an eviction notice too.

"Yes, I've got one as well. Let me ring around and see if everyone else has them," said Josie, mostly to buy herself time, as she needed that cup of tea and a shower before she dealt with yet another crisis.

Everyone she spoke to had also received an eviction letter and were equally incensed, but it was Kara who perhaps made sense of why they had received them.

"I think Smythe needs to have vacant possession for the sale to go through," she said.

"I think you're right," replied Josie. "Perhaps he's been playing a game all along, knowing we wouldn't pay for non-existent services in order to have an excuse to evict us!"

"It wouldn't stand up in court, though, would it Josie?" said Kara.

"No. However, he's probably gambling on the fact we wouldn't have the money to take the council to court."

"Yes, and by the time we got organised, our allotments would already have been bulldozed!" said Kara, dourly.

Ben had come up with much the same theory, but also had some interesting information for Kara.

"After I cleaned up that image for Jack, I cleaned up the audio track too, getting rid of the background noise so I could hear it better. I listened to it through headphones, over and over again until I got a full transcript" he said.

"And?" asked Josie.

"Smythe was telling Gilbert that Hawk were paying £5 million for the land, but that he was going to tell the council it was £4 million," he replied.

"So, they were pocketing a million?" said Josie, incredulously.

"Yes, that's right. Smythe was telling Poppy they would have £500,000 each."

"Wow - no wonder they are keen!" Josie replied. "Seeing as we obtained this information perhaps illegally, let's keep that to ourselves for now and see what Jack and Kara come up with on Friday."

Ben agreed and they said their goodbyes, then Josie rang John again to reassure him that they weren't the only ones to be evicted and to outline Kara's theory, which John felt was a plausible explanation.

"I hope you don't mind, but I've been talking to Sarah," John said. "I'm going to bring her to our meeting on Saturday. If we have a fight on our hands, she's a lot of experience that can help us."

"Oh?" said Josie, intrigued.

"She was an environmental activist working for Greenpeace, until she broke her back falling from the *Rainbow Warrior*."

"Oh, poor woman," exclaimed Josie.

"She wouldn't want your sympathy, Josie, she's very much of the 'one door closes, another door opens' frame of mind," said John.

"She sounds amazing!" said Josie.

"Yes," agreed John, "she is pretty special. I'm enjoying getting to know her."

"I'm so pleased, John," said Josie, sincerely, whilst trying to supress a stab of jealousy.

"Me too, Josie," agreed John, "but she'll never replace my Mary!"

John went on to say that he'd spoken to Hugo, who was on holiday in France, but that as soon as he was home, he would ring round all his council contacts and see what he could find out. Hugo was very clear that faking consultation with those affected by a proposed development was illegal and would show that there was some corruption going on.

"Well, I think we're all pretty clear who the corrupt councillor is!" said Josie.

# CHAPTER FIFTY-TWO

"I think this is the pub," said Jack, as he and Kara stood outside the Fox and Grapes in a smart area of Leeds.

"It's several years ago now and the sign looks like it's new, but the pub was certainly on this corner," he concluded.

Once Jack had seen the enhanced picture, he'd been certain that the man Poppy Gilbert had met with at the allotments was Julian Fernsby, and if he'd got the right pub, this was Julian's favourite drinking place. There was no guarantee he'd be there, but with not much more than a week before the council meeting to decide the fate of the allotments, Jack had his fingers crossed that their gamble would pay off.

Josie was staying with the children overnight and she'd picked them up from school so that Jack and Kara could set off in good time. They had got to Leeds a couple of hours ago and checked into a local B&B and then checked out the king-sized bed before a quick shower and change before going onto the pub. Kara was relaxed and happy, feeling almost on holiday, but Jack was a little on edge, knowing how much was riding on this weekend.

Jack heard Julian before he saw him, recognising his braying laugh, and a quick glance confirmed it was him. He was sitting amongst a loose group of, what appeared to be, pub regulars, their table piled with full and empty pint glasses. Jack and Kara ordered drinks and took them to a table near to where Julian was sitting, deliberately ignoring him, but sitting so that Jack was in Julian's line of sight. They sipped their drinks and waited, hoping Julian would recognise Jack.

"Jack, is that you? Jack Brown?" Julian suddenly shouted.

Jack turned to look and then jumped up and took the few steps towards him, holding out his hand.

"Julian! How nice to see you," said Jack, shaking his hand.

"Kara," Jack called. "Come and meet my old friend, Julian."

Julian's eyebrows shot up.

"New filly, Jack?" he stage-whispered.

"Yes, but don't tell the wife!" Jack replied.

"A man after my own heart!" said Julian, slapping him on the back before kissing Kara on the cheek.

Having seen the video, Kara had to try hard not to cringe, especially when Julian's hand slipped from her shoulder to her bottom. They made small talk for a moment and then she excused herself to go to the ladies, aware of Julian's eyes on her as she walked across the pub.

"Nice arse on that, Jack!" he said.

Jack had to restrain himself from punching him and sat quickly on a vacant chair across the table, his clenched fists hidden from view.

"What the fuck happened to you, Jack?" asked Julian. "I rung your company to get your help on a deal I was working on, and they said you had gone. Couldn't, or wouldn't, tell me where!"

"I moved up towards the North Yorkshire Moors and I'm running my own landscaping business," said Jack, deliberately bending the truth a little to lead Julian where he wanted him.

"Really?" exclaimed Julian. "That's a change of direction! Bit of a midlife crisis?"

"Well, I'm a bit young for that, but, yeah, sort of," replied Jack.

"Explains the fit bird then," said Julian with a leer. "Like them a bit older myself – know what they're doing, if you know what I mean."

"Yeah, I do know what you mean," replied Jack, images from the video flashing into his mind.

"It's early days yet, I'm still getting established," continued Jack. "I could do with a big bit of work to take me to the next level."

"Well, I might be able to help you there," replied Julian. "We're just about to start a big housing development up your way and you're welcome to tender for the landscaping part."

"Wow, that would be great!" said Jack, picking up Julian's empty glass. "Let me get them in and then you can tell me all about it."

When Jack came back with the brimming pints of beer, Kara had returned and had said something to make Julian laugh.

"Hi love," said Jack, resisting the need to put his arm around her and pull her close. "Julian was just about to tell me about some work he might be able to put my way."

"Yeah," replied Julian, taking a long drink from the glass Jack handed him. "Business is all about who you know. I heard about this opportunity from someone my father plays golf with, and he knew about it from this tart. Cor, she was a goer – a pleasure to do business with!"

Kara was miming being sick behind Julian's back, and Jack struggled to keep a straight face.

"Whereabouts is it, mate?" asked Jack.

"It's the site of former allotments in Kirkby. Do you know it?" said Julian.

"Yes, I know it well," replied Jack, truthfully. "Great views."

"Yeah, that's going to be a big selling point," said Julian.

"Sounds lovely," said Kara. "I wouldn't mind buying one there!"

"Well, you'll need the best part of a million to buy one, love," replied Julian, puffing out his chest.

"Gosh, well I think that counts me out," replied Kara.

"You must have paid a lot for the land then, Julian, for the houses to be so expensive," said Jack.

"Well, they are going to be 'executive' houses, none of this 'affordable shit', but I got it for a song. Just seven mil and I'm building 30 houses at around one mil each. You do the maths, Jack, but I'm going to do very well out of this one!" said Julian with a big grin.

"Wow, you certainly are!" replied Jack, "But are you sure you'll get planning permission? They're a bit picky around there about new developments, especially on previously unbuilt land."

"Not a problem Jack," replied Julian, banging down his now empty glass. "As I said, it's who you know. This golfing buddy of my fathers is on the Council and he's pulling strings for us. Of course, I'm having to make it worth his while, by quite a big chunk actually, but it'll be well worth it."

"Right, I'll get them in, shall I? Drink up," said Julian, nodding at Jack's half full glass.

"Not for me, thanks Julian. We have a table booked for dinner and have to dash. I'll give you a call about that tender, shall I? Still the same number?" said Jack.

They said their goodbyes, and as Jack and Kara emerged into the welcome cool of the night air, Jack let out a long breath, relieved to be outside and away from Julian. Kara put her hand into her bag and pulled out her phone, checked it carefully and then switched off the recording.

"Got it!" she said with a grin.

"Kara!" exclaimed Jack. "You are a star!"

"I was just following Zoe's instructions," she replied, tucking her arm through his. "Now, I think dinner was mentioned. Come on, I'm starving!"

# CHAPTER FIFTY-THREE

After a morning's shopping, Jack was very pleased to be on their way home. Although he'd lived in Leeds for most of his life, the tall buildings and crush of people now made him feel claustrophobic; the closer they got to the rolling hills and open fields of North Yorkshire, the better he felt. They'd split up to shop, Kara wanting to get something secretly for Jack's upcoming birthday and Jack having his own surprise to buy. Kara was pleased to have found the exact trainers that Ronan had been nagging her about for weeks and had got a new book for Lily by her favourite author.

Jack was driving, so Kara closed her eyes and nodded off a bit, only waking when the smooth surface of the A64 turned into roller coaster of The Avenue, the grand processional approach to Castle Howard.

"Oh, you've come the pretty way," exclaimed Kara, "I love this road!"

"Me too," said Jack, slowing down so that they could gaze up at the first of the architectural markers along the way, a tall stone column crowned with a gilded brazier that shone brightly in the autumn sunshine.

The trees opened out to reveal ahead the first 'gate', a short line of crenelated stone walls with a central arch, a mock fortification that welcomed you onwards. As they passed through the gate, they glimpsed the pyramid arch of the next gate beyond the humps and hollows of the road. The beech trees in thick formation between the two gates were glorious in their rich autumn colours, the rows of shimmering tree continuing past the gates and on to the horizon.

Beyond the next gatehouse arch the land rose up towards a giant obelisk, standing proud on the horizon in the middle of a mini roundabout. Driving around this, Kara was surprised that Jack turned right, taking the road towards Castle Howard itself, the grand house glimpsed now for the first time.

"Oh, are we stopping?" she asked. "Don't we need to get back for the children and the meeting?"

"We do," replied Jack, "but we've plenty of time, so I thought we'd stretch our legs and steal a few more moments alone, if that's okay?"

"More than okay with me," said Kara, taking his hand as they walked towards the entrance to the grounds.

Hand in hand they strolled around the lake, enjoying the view of the magnificent house mirrored in water that was ablaze with the reflection of autumnal trees. Cutting through the woods, leaves crunching under foot, they made their way to the stunning Temple of the Four Winds. They walked slowly around it, stopping between the statues on each side, following their stony gaze across acres of stunning parkland and rolling countryside. Jack thought this might be the perfect place and felt in his pocket for the small box he had picked up in Leeds, but a noisy family of four and their boisterous dog bounded up, and the moment was lost.

Coming back past the house, Jack suggested that they look at the walled garden, which was a more intimate world, a change from the grandeur of lakes and monuments. The borders were full of flowers they knew, and they wandered round happily, feeling at home. Jack led Kara to a curved white bench, secluded within a high hedge, and they kissed, hidden from view.

"I love you, Kara," said Jack, looking deep into her eyes.

"And I love you, Jack. Being with you makes me very happy," replied Kara.

She moved in to kiss him again, but Jack was already moving to stand up, before sinking to his knees in front of her. Kara gasped as he held out a box in which nestled a ring sparkling in the sunlight.

"Will you marry me, Kara?" Jack said simply.

"Yes," was all she replied, too busy kissing him to say more.

Jack took the ring out of the box and slipped it onto her finger, anxious that it might not fit. He had traced around a ring in her jewellery box when she was in the shower one day, but it was still a relief to find it fitted her perfectly.

"You can change it if you don't like it," said Jack, anxiously.

"I love it!" Kara replied, holding her hand up and twisting it from side to side to admire the large solitaire diamond nestled between white gold shoulders engraved with entwined flowers. "It's absolutely perfect. Thank you," she said before kissing him again.

Jack knew that his great-grandma's magnificent diamond and sapphire ring would be his one day, and that when that happened, he would give it to Kara, but he wanted to give her something he had chosen and paid for, and he'd saved almost all the money he had made through gardening that year to buy it.

As they walked hand in hand back to the car, a text pinged in from Josie telling them that she was at the allotment with the children, picking strawberries, and that she would take them up to the manor ready for their return. Even though it had only been one night, Kara had missed the children dreadfully, and as soon as they got back, she dashed to find them, pulling them both into a bear hug. Kara and Jack had agreed to speak to the children before they told anyone else, so they took them into Jack's little sitting room and told them their good news.

Ronan put his hands on his hips and looked at Jack seriously.

"Will you be kind to mummy and not make her cry like daddy did?" he asked.

"I promise," said Jack, shaking hands solemnly with Ronan.

"Oh Ronan!" said Josie giving him a big hug.

"Will you be my daddy now?" asked Lily, sucking her thumb and looking confused.

"Well Lily, you are a very lucky girl as you will have two daddies, Daddy Andy and Daddy Jack. We both love you very much, and just because I'm marrying your mummy doesn't stop Daddy Andy from being your daddy too," said Jack, kneeling down to Lily's height.

Lily threw her arms around his neck, nearly causing him to topple over.

"I love you, Daddy Jack!"

"I love you too, Munchkin," he said, tears welling in his eyes.

Kara dragged Ronan into a group hug, and Jack felt a surge of joy that he now was going to be part of a family. Snacks were made for everyone, and then the children were settled in front of a TV with the door open whilst Kara and Jack joined the others in Dorothy's large sitting room. Although they had serious matters to discuss, once they had announced their happy news Dorothy insisted on opening a bottle of champagne to toast the happy couple.

Everyone wished them happiness and admired the ring, so it was a little while before the meeting got started, and by that time the unaccustomed champagne had put Dorothy to sleep, and she was snoring lightly. Jack tucked a blanket over her knees and then brought everyone up to date on the meeting with Julian in the pub the previous night.

"How much?" asked Ben after a moment's stunned silence.

"Seven million," confirmed Kara. "Listen." Kara played the recording on her phone, and they listened in astonishment.

"Wow." said Zoe. "He must have been very drunk to confess all that to you!"

"Just arrogant, I think," said Jack. "People with money often think the law doesn't apply to them!"

"Well," said Ben, "that's really interesting because Smythe told Gilbert that he was being paid five million, but that he was telling the council it was four million, so that they could pocket the difference, fifty – fifty."

"Except," said Sarah, "if I understand correctly, he was being paid seven million, so he was pocketing an extra two million on top!"

"The lying, thieving bastard!" exclaimed Kara, loudly. "Making two and a half million on the sale of the allotment!"

"Who's selling the allotments?" asked Dorothy, waking up with a start.

"The council are, Great-Grandma," said Jack.

"Well, they can't!" she replied crossly.

"We're going to do our best to stop them, Dorothy," said Josie, patting her hand.

"You don't need to; they can't sell the land!" Dorothy replied.

"Why's that, Dorothy?" asked Kara.

"Because it's not theirs to sell!" she replied.

Kara glanced at Jack, hoping Dorothy wasn't becoming confused in her old age, but Jack was looking at his great-grandma with nothing but curiosity on his face.

"Whose land is it, Great-Grandma?" he asked.

"Why, mine of course!" she replied.

"But I thought you gave it to the council!" said Kara.

"No, they rent them. I wanted to keep the land in the family, well, just in case, so they pay me a peppercorn rent for it – £5 a year. It's been in place so long they have probably forgotten it, but I check every January that the rent has been paid, and it was this year, the same as always."

"Do you think Smythe knew?" said Zoe.

"Oh, he knows alright," replied Dorothy. "The annual cheque for £5 has his signature on it!"

"How on earth did he think he'd get away with it?" asked Sarah.

"Oh, I expect he's just hoping I'll die very soon," replied Dorothy, cheerfully.

# CHAPTER FIFTY-FOUR

The double doors of the council chamber flew open with a bang, interrupting Councillor Smythe in full flow.

"I thought I said there were to be no interruptions!" he thundered.

Everyone stared at the doorway, as slowly, leaning heavily on Jack's Arm on one side and Kara's on the other, Lady Dorothy Kirkby entered the room. Right behind them were Josie and two police officers who closed the doors and stood in front of them. Dorothy wore a long midnight blue satin dress, a fur stole and a small tiara, an outfit that on anyone else would have looked ridiculous, but on her looked just right.

For a moment no one moved, then a Councillor jumped up and hurriedly fetched her a chair. Jack, Kara and Josie found their own chairs against the wall and sat back to enjoy the show.

"Lady Kirkby," said Councillor Smythe icily, "I wasn't aware you were attending this meeting."

"And I wasn't aware of the meeting, Smythe," she said haughtily. "Someone omitted to invite me!"

"In the circumstances, madam, there was no point inviting you!" responded Smythe.

"No point? Are you not discussing the sale of the land on which the allotments stand?" she asked.

"We are, but seeing as you gave it to the Council nearly 70 years ago, it is no longer your concern, so therefore no point in you being here," said Smythe, speaking slowly, as if speaking to a small child.

"Now, if you will excuse us, we have important business to discuss," he said, before turning to his secretary and flapping his hands in Jack and Kara's general direction. "Escort Lady Kirkby and these people out."

Dorothy settled herself more comfortably in her chair. "I did not *give* it to the council, Smythe, I leased it to them on a peppercorn rent," she said.

There was a sharp intake of breath, making it obvious that several in the room were unaware of that fact.

"Yes, yes," replied Smythe, dismissively, "but in case you have forgotten, in the terms of the lease the land would become the Council's property once 70 years had elapsed or upon your death, whichever was soonest."

"There is nothing wrong with my memory, Smythe, but correct me if I'm wrong, but neither eventuality has yet occurred!" Dorothy responded.

"No, not yet, but at nearly hundred years old, I think it's safe to assume that the latter condition will shortly become true, and if not, the former condition will apply soon enough," he replied coldly.

"Well, as neither currently apply, aren't you being a bit premature, Smythe, in selling off my land?"

"Just getting the ball rolling, Lady Kirkby. The people of Kirkby need houses and we are just trying to help," Smythe said sanctimoniously.

"Trying to help 'the people', Smythe, or trying to help yourself?" asked Dorothy, icily.

"I don't know what you are talking about, Madam, but I warn you, you will be speaking to my solicitor if you are making allegations that will damage my good name," spluttered Smythe.

Dorothy ignored the red-faced Smythe and turned to the rest of the Councillors.

"Ladies and Gentlemen," she said loudly, "I understand that the price Smythe says you have been offered for my land is four million pounds, give or take: is that correct?"

Several people nodded their heads, all too in awe of Lady Kirkby to actually speak.

"Well, it may come as a surprise to you, but the price actually being paid is seven million pounds. There is a small 'sweetener', I think the phrase is, being paid to Smythe and his harlot," she said nodding toward Poppy.

There was an audible gasp and then pandemonium broke out. Poppy rushed at Smythe and started to hit him indiscriminately, screaming at him for trying to diddle her out of her fair share.

"He was obviously screwing her in more ways than one!" Kara commented sotto voce to Jack.

The police officers grabbed Poppy, twisted her arms behind her back and slapped on handcuffs before one of them dragged her out of the room; the sound of her cursing and swearing echoing back long after she had gone.

"That is a lie!" exploded Smyth. "This is defamation of character, and you have no evidence to back it up!"

"Ah, but we do, Councillor," said Josie, stepping forward and handing a file to the Leader of the Council.

"She can't prove anything," spat out Smythe, turning to his colleagues, "and besides, the old bat will be dead soon and the land will be ours."

"I accept that I am not long for this world," Dorothy said cheerfully, "but in all other aspects you are incorrect, Smythe. Firstly, we have plenty of evidence of you and Pauline Gilbert conspiring to defraud the Council, including video of your, umm, 'liaison'. Secondly there is a clause in the lease that you are apparently unaware of: that is, on my death or at the end of 70 years, the land passes back to my descendants to do with as they wish."

"Ha, ha, Lady Kirkby, I think it's a bit late for that, don't you?" he sneered.

Dorothy smiled and raised an eyebrow, before extended a hand towards Jack, who came forward and took her hand.

"Councillor Smythe, let me introduce you to my great-grandson, Jack Henry Neville-Brown," said Dorothy, as Jack leant in and kissed her cheek.

# CHAPTER FIFTY-FIVE

After Smythe was arrested and removed from the council chamber, the Leader of the Council fell over backwards to apologise to Lady Kirkby and assured her that he had no idea of Smythe's deception. Dorothy fixed him with a gimlet eye and admonished him for failing to undertake 'due diligence', before she swept out of the room, leaving the poor man almost in tears.

By the time the four of them got back to Dorothy's apartment, the adrenaline had drained out of her and exhaustion had taken over. Josie helped her to bed, but Dorothy insisted that they open a 'good' bottle of champagne to celebrate with her, but she was fast asleep before they even had time to bring her a glass.

The three friends sat looking out of the French windows at the allotments, sipping their champagne and discussing the day. They were all feeling exuberant, but Josie still had one question that was worrying her.

"Jack, once the land is yours, will you sell it? Will we still have allotments?" she eventually asked.

"Yes and no, Josie," he replied. "Great-Grandma and I have discussed it at length, and we have both agreed on a plan. Smythe was right that we do need more houses in Kirkby: not the big, executive, detached houses that he was planning, but affordable houses. For a long time, I couldn't afford a home of my own and there are lots of people on the streets who can only dream of a place of their own. If it hadn't been for you two, I would probably still be homeless. We need starter homes for young people, homes suitable for people with disabilities, houses for single parents where their children can play safely, houses suitable for elderly people that don't shut them off from life."

Jack paused for breath, and Kara squeezed his hand.

"However, the mental and physical benefits of having an allotment can't be underestimated. My plan is to do both, to use half the land for a small community of homes built in a square around an enclosed communal garden. Somewhere where children can play, adults can sit and chat, flowers and vegetables can be grown and enjoyed by all. These will be available on a low rent, subsidised by the interest from the fund great-grandma set up nearly 70 years ago, rather than that money be for the allotments, as we feel this is a better use of the money."

Josie nodded in agreement.

"Above the houses, allotments for anyone in Kirkby to use, continued Jack. "It would halve the number of allotments available, but currently many of the allotments are underutilised – folk that like the idea, but not the hard work! I think there would be enough left for the dedicated gardeners. What do you think?"

"I think it's amazing," said Josie, "absolutely brilliant! Just one thing, will Mary's Memorial Allotments remain?"

"Of course," replied Jack, "that won't be touched. The children's garden will be moved from its current location to where Ms Gilbert's plot was, so we can use the barn as a teaching space when the weather's poor, and I'll run it into my current plot so we can have a bigger sensory garden. I'll put a gate through from the manor garden so we can take Dorothy to enjoy the sensory garden and so she can sit in the barn and reminisce. Obviously, all this is a long way off, I've got to find a sympathetic architect and get planning permission first, so your job's safe for a lot longer!"

"Sadly!" said Josie dryly, and they all laughed.

They chatted a bit longer about Jack's plan, getting caught up in his excitement. Eventually Josie got up to go, leaving the two lovebirds, as she called them, alone to watch the sunset over the allotments. Each leaf and stem were edged with gold which deepened to red before the sky faded into indigo and the individual plots became just one darkly patterned carpet.

"I love this view," said Kara, snuggling up to Jack on the window seat.

Jack smiled at her and kissed her forehead.

"Would you like to live here after we are married?" he asked.

"I think the children would be a bit too much for Dorothy," laughed Kara.

"Ah, no, I should explain. There is a four-bedroom apartment on the top floor, the penthouse I think they call it, that has just come free. great-grandma asked if we wanted it," said Jack.

"Wow! That would be amazing," said Kara, her eyes shining.

"The views from there are incredible; you can see over the whole town and across to the hills beyond and watch the sun rise and set every day," Jack continued enthusiastically.

"Yes, that would be great, but I was thinking more about the fourth bedroom…" she said, looking into his eyes.

"What! Oh!" said Jack, suddenly realising what she meant. He pulled her close and kissed her passionately.

"I think we'd better start planning our wedding, sooner rather than later, before I get any fatter," she said when they eventually surfaced.

"I was thinking the same, actually," said Jack, suddenly serious.

"What! That I'm fat?" exclaimed Kara, thumping him on the arm.

"Ouch! No, sorry, I didn't mean that. No, I was thinking of Dorothy: I want her to be at our wedding, and she really isn't getting any younger. She was magnificent today, but was exhausted afterwards, and well, I don't know how much longer we will have her. She's had such a sad life and I want her to have some joy before she goes," said Jack sadly.

Kara smiled warmly and squeezed his hand. "I always fancied a Christmas wedding," she said.

# EPILOGUE

The ancient parish church always looked lovely at Christmas, with festive arrangements of holly, ivy and spruce on the windowsills and a large Christmas tree lit by simple white lights in the porch. For Jack and Kara's wedding, Josie had put lots of red altar candles amongst the foliage and hundreds of tea-lights around the tops of the old stone pillars. She had woven tiny white fairy lights around the intricate carving of the chancel screen and altar rail and tied bunches of festive greenery with red satin ribbon to the ends of all the pews.

The most difficult bit had been constructing a bridal arch of holly, ivy, spruce and mistletoe around the outside of the curved entrance to the porch. Ben had made her a wire frame which he had secured to the lantern above the arch; it wasn't particularly stable, but as long as it wasn't windy it would remain standing. Josie had woven red ribbon and a few white roses into the greenery and had been was very happy with the finished arch.

Whilst they waited in anticipation for the arrival of the bride, the organist played a medley of Christmas carols and the guests chatted quietly to friends and family in the pews around them. Much to Jack's surprise, the church was full. He had worried that Dorothy would be the only occupant of the 'groom's side' of the church, but friends from the allotments, some of Dorothy's newly found relatives and some of the children from his classes and their parents had filled it out nicely.

He was touched to see that his ex-wife, Julie, with her partner, Nathan, and their beautiful baby daughter had come too: they were sitting towards the back where they could make a quick exit if the baby woke and started to cry. Dorothy had been quite shocked that his ex-wife was there, but Jack had explained to her that they were never really anything more than best friends, and that friendship remained once he had been able to forgive her. Besides, if things hadn't worked out the way they had, he wouldn't be marrying Kara who was the love of his life.

Dorothy sat regally in the front row, magnificent in a large hat with an arching ostrich feather that obscured the view of all those seated behind her. They had brought her as far as the door in a wheelchair, but she had insisted she would walk into the church, so with Jack on one side and Ben, Jack's best man, on the other ("my handsome young men" she called them), she slowly made her way down the aisle, waving regally as she passed other members of the congregation.

Ronan had refused to be a pageboy, and was an usher, under Ben's watchful eye, wearing a red waistcoat to match the groom and best man's. Lily had been delighted to be a bridesmaid and was joined by her cousins Skye and Zara: Jack could only imagine the girly mayhem that was taking place at home and was glad that Zoe had been persuaded to be the chief bridesmaid to keep them all in order.

He knew from Lily that the bridesmaids were wearing 'sticky-out' white dresses with red sashes, but Kara's red dress would be a surprise. If he'd thought about what she was wearing at all, he had probably imagined she would be in white, but she could have worn a bin liner and he wouldn't have cared; she would still be beautiful to him.

Josie sat on her own, listening to the music and enjoying the atmosphere of happy anticipation. Tomorrow was Christmas Day and she was joining the happy couple, Dorothy, Ben and Zoe and John and Sarah at Kirkby Manor for Christmas lunch. She thought back to the previous year when she had spent Christmas Day on her own, and to the many years before when she had spent it with Keith.

She realised that she had still been grieving last year, which was why she'd turned down invitations from Kara and others to join them for Christmas, thinking that she would need to get used to spending Christmas on her own. She examined her feelings now and realised that her grief had moved on from melancholy to happy memories of Keith, and she was finally ready to embrace whatever fate threw her way.

"Is this seat taken?" asked a man.

Josie looked up and was momentary dazzled as sunlight through the stained glass threw multi-coloured lights around a tall man standing uncertainly at the end of the pew.

As he moved slightly out of the light, she could see his face, which looked kind, with a few lines that showed he smiled more than frowned. He was tall with clear blue eyes and iron-grey hair that was thick and wavy. Josie felt a sudden jolt of recognition, and maybe he felt the same, as he smiled and held out his hand, and when she held hers out to him, he closed his other hand over hers and a warmth flowed through her.

"Hello," he said, "my name's Hugo."

Jean Illingworth

# THE END

# Disclaimer

The fictional town of Kirkby is based upon the friendly North Yorkshire town of Kirkbymoorside, which does have some splendid allotments on the hill above the town. However, Kirkby Manor does not exist and all people and events in this book are fictitious: any similarity to events or to people alive or dead are purely coincidental.

# Acknowledgements

Many thanks to the Kirkbymoorside Allotment Association and all their allotment holders, who were a great help when researching this book. None of the events in this book occurred there, but I'm sure they have their own stories to tell.

# About the Author

Jean Illingworth lives in North Yorkshire with her husband, DJ, and son, Jamie. She has written several books for children and young adults, most of them illustrated by Jamie, but this is her first novel for adults. When not writing, Jean enjoys photographing the stunning Yorkshire coast and countryside, is a passionate gardener, and enjoys singing and socialising with family and friends.

# Other Books by Jean Illingworth

Danny's Bonfire Night

Danny's Christmas

Dragontide

Danny's Easter

Danny's Summer Holiday

Beach Beings

Beach Beings – Distant Shores

Two Degrees